You're A Privileged Woman.

INTRODUCING
PAGES & PRIVILEGES™.

It's our way of thanking you for buying
our books at your favorite retail store.

─── *GET ALL THIS FREE* ───
WITH JUST ONE PROOF OF PURCHASE:

◆ **Hotel Discounts** up
to 60% at home and
abroad ◆ **Travel Service**
- Guaranteed lowest
published airfares
plus 5% cash back
on tickets ◆ **$25 Travel Voucher**

$50 VALUE

◆ **Sensuous Petite Parfumerie** collection

◆ **Insider Tips Letter**
with sneak previews
of upcoming books

You'll get a FREE personal card, too.
It's your passport to all these benefits– and to
even more great gifts & benefits to come!
There's no club to join. No purchase commitment. No obligation.

Enrollment Form

☐ *Yes!* I WANT TO BE A *Privileged Woman.*

Enclosed is one *PAGES & PRIVILEGES*™ Proof of Purchase from any Harlequin or Silhouette book currently for sale in stores (Proofs of Purchase are found on the back pages of books) and the store cash register receipt. Please enroll me in *PAGES & PRIVILEGES*™. Send my Welcome Kit and FREE Gifts -- and activate my FREE benefits -- immediately.

More great gifts and benefits to come like these luxurious Truly Lace and L'Effleur gift baskets. ▶

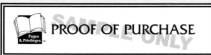

▶ DETACH HERE AND MAIL TODAY!

NAME (please print)
_____

ADDRESS _____ APT. NO _____

CITY _____ STATE _____ ZIP/POSTAL CODE _____

PROOF OF PURCHASE
Pages & Privileges™	SAMPLE ONLY

Please allow 6-8 weeks for delivery. Quantities are limited. We reserve the right to substitute items. Enroll before October 31, 1995 and receive one full year of benefits.

NO CLUB!
NO COMMITMENT!
Just one purchase brings you great **Free Gifts and Benefits!**
(More details in back of this book.)

Name of store where this book was purchased_____

Date of purchase_____

Type of store:

☐ Bookstore   ☐ Supermarket   ☐ Drugstore

☐ Dept. or discount store (e.g. K-Mart or Walmart)

☐ Other (specify)_____

Which Harlequin or Silhouette series do you usually read?
_____

Pages & Privileges™

Complete and mail with one Proof of Purchase and store receipt to:

U.S.: *PAGES & PRIVILEGES*™, P.O. Box 1960, Danbury, CT 06813-1960

Canada: *PAGES & PRIVILEGES*™, 49-6A The Donway West, P.O. 813, North York, ON M3C 2E8   **PRINTED IN U.S.A**

The Story So Far…

After her father's death, Gemma Smith made two astonishing discoveries: amongst his possessions she found a priceless black opal, and an old photograph that made her believe that she could be nearly twenty—almost two years older than her father had led her to believe. Gemma decided to leave the Outback to find out more about her mother, who had died when she was born, and to start a new life.

Fate introduced her to Nathan Whitmore, a successful screenwriter and the acting head of Whitmore Opals. Highly attracted to Gemma and struck by her vulnerability, Nathan offered her a reward for the black opal, which he suspected had been stolen from Byron Whitmore, his adoptive father, more than twenty years before. Nathan also offered Gemma a home and jobs in Sydney—first as "minder" to his wayward teenage daughter, Kirsty, and then, when Gemma had mastered Japanese, on the sales force of Whitmore Opals. Gemma found herself falling for her new protector, although various members of the Whitmore household warned her that Nathan was a heartless seducer.

But, to her delight, Nathan proposed marriage, though Gemma still had her doubts: she may have been about to become the second Mrs. Nathan Whitmore, but did she really know her husband-to-be…and what about the intriguing secrets of her real origins, and the black opal?

Dear Reader,

Welcome to a new and totally compelling family saga, set in the glamorous, cutthroat world of opal dealing in Australia.

Laden with dark secrets, forbidden desires, scandalous discoveries and happy endings, Hearts of Fire unfolds over a series of six books, from now until December. Beautiful, innocent Gemma Smith goes in search of a new life, and fate introduces her to Nathan Whitmore, the ruthless, talented and utterly controlled screenwriter and acting head of Whitmore Opals.

Throughout the series, Gemma will discover the truth about Nathan, seduction, her real mother and the priceless Black Opal. But, at the same time, in each novel you'll find an independent, fully developed romance that can be read on its own, revealing the passion, deception and hope that has existed between two fabulously rich clans over twenty tempestuous years.

Hearts of Fire has been especially written by one of romance fiction's rising stars for you to enjoy—we're sure you will.

The Editor

MIRANDA LEE

Desire & Deception

HEARTS
OF
FIRE
2

Harlequin Books

TORONTO • NEW YORK • LONDON
AMSTERDAM • PARIS • SYDNEY • HAMBURG
STOCKHOLM • ATHENS • TOKYO • MILAN
MADRID • WARSAW • BUDAPEST • AUCKLAND

ISBN 0-373-11760-4

DESIRE & DECEPTION

First North American Publication 1995.

Copyright © 1994 by Miranda Lee.

PRINCIPAL CHARACTERS IN THIS BOOK

GEMMA SMITH-WHITMORE: after her father's death, Gemma discovers a magnificent black opal worth a small fortune and an old photograph that casts doubt on her real identity. In quest of the truth and a new life, she goes to Sydney, and fate introduces her to Nathan Whitmore, her husband-to-be....

NATHAN WHITMORE: adopted son of Byron Whitmore, Nathan is acting head of Whitmore Opals and a talented screenwriter. After a troubled childhood and a divorce, he is ruthless and utterly emotionally controlled. Will he ever drop that mask and give Gemma the love that she needs...?

JADE WHITMORE: the spoiled, willful only daughter of Byron and the late Irene Whitmore (née Campbell). Her wild-child ways give the wrong impression to everyone except, perhaps, Kyle Armstrong?

KYLE ARMSTRONG: the new marketing manager at Whitmore Opals. He is unforthcoming about his background—does he plan to use the Whitmore family for his own ends?

BYRON WHITMORE: recently widowed, he is the head of the Whitmore family, and a stranger to love.

LENORE LANGTRY: talented stage actress, ex-wife of Nathan Whitmore and mother of Kirsty, Lenore has finally found love with top lawyer, Zachary Marsden.

MELANIE LLOYD: housekeeper to the Whitmores, Melanie has been on emotional autopilot since the tragic deaths of her husband and only child.

AVA WHITMORE: Byron's much-younger sister, she struggles with her weight, her unmarried state and her fear of failure.

KIRSTY WHITMORE: the wayward fourteen-year-old daughter of Nathan and Lenore.

FAMILY TREE

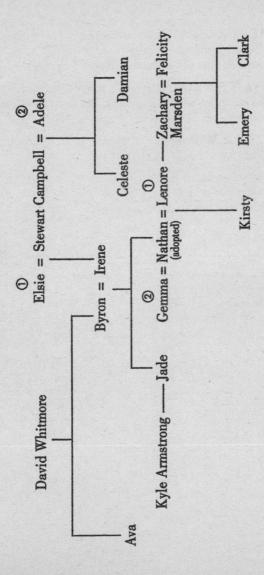

CHAPTER ONE

JADE woke to daylight and confusion.

Where on earth am I? she wondered fuzzily, her head thick with the after-effects of sleeping tablets.

And then she remembered.

She was back in her old bedroom at Belleview. Back home.

'Oh, God,' she groaned, and rolled out of bed, clutching her pounding temples while she staggered, naked, across the white shag carpet and into her white and gold *en-suite* bathroom.

'Oh, *God*,' she groaned again when she saw her reflection in the mirror. Her short white-blonde hair was sticking out in all directions, her dark blue eyes like black holes in her pasty face.

But it was her bruised breasts that drew and held her attention. She hadn't realised...

Jade stared at them for a long moment before shuddering violently. Suddenly, the full horror of what she'd narrowly escaped hit her, and she sank down on the side of the bath, her head dropping down between her knees as the nausea rose from her stomach. For a few seconds, the room spun, but the moment passed. Jade braced herself with hands on knees and slowly lifted her head. She still felt a little clammy and decided to sit there for a while longer.

Her thoughts kept going round, however. Regretful, recriminating thoughts.

She shouldn't have agreed to let Roberto use the spare room of her unit till he could find a place of his own. She definitely shouldn't have agreed to his holding a small party last night.

But in truth, she hadn't seen any danger. After all, Roberto was gay. And so were all his friends. Jade had always found gay men not only sweet, but kind and gentlemanly and very interesting to talk to. They made good friends for women. Safe friends.

But one of Roberto's friends had not been safe.

The horror washed in again, bringing another wave of nausea.

Jade stood up abruptly and walked over to the shower, snapping on the water and standing there testing till it was hot enough. Stepping into the steaming spray, she shut her eyes and turned her face upwards, closing her mind to everything but the steady beating of its cleansing, reviving heat.

It was a mental trick she had learnt long ago. When things got too painful, she just clicked off her thoughts to everything but the most immediate and superficial needs. Washing. Eating. Sleeping.

For the first time, it didn't work. She couldn't seem to forget that hand over her mouth, that steely arm clamped around her breasts, those filthy words whispered in her ear. If she hadn't managed that lucky kick to her assailant's groin, God knew what would have happened.

But she had, and unexpectedly she'd been free. Snatching up her car keys from the hall table, she'd bolted for the door, wearing nothing but a silk robe, driving home to Belleview at a speed which owed thanks to its being three o'clock in the morning, with the streets of suburban Sydney almost deserted. Heaven knew what would have happened if she'd been stopped by the police. God, she could see it now, being arrested for dangerous driving and hauled, half-naked down to the police station. Then a sour-faced Nathan arriving the following morning with the family solicitor in tow. Like the last time.

Only the last time her arrest had been for possession of drugs. Zachary Marsden had defended her on that occasion as well.

Of course, it hadn't been *her* marijuana in the glovebox of her car. She detested drugs. It had belonged to a so-called friend who'd vowed she'd given up the habit. Luckily, Zachary was a top defender—would her father employ any other kind?—and he'd soon proved her innocence to the satisfaction of the magistrate and the charges had been dropped. Zachary had really believed in her innocence, too, which was more than could be said for Nathan.

What a hypocrite her adopted brother was!

He pretended to be holier-than-thou, just like her father. But she knew what he'd been up to before Byron found him on the streets of King's Cross. Yet he had the hide to judge her over her supposedly loose lifestyle, to criticise her for being sexually provocative.

Jade had to laugh at that. Nathan oozed sex. Why, there wasn't a woman within fifty feet of him who hadn't wanted him at some stage, her own mother included.

Immediately, Jade's mind closed in on the subject of her mother. In her opinion, she hadn't had a mother. End of story.

Back to Nathan.

Jade switched off the shower, her generous mouth curving into a bitter smile. She had that cold-blooded devil taped, all right. People felt sorry for him because of his supposedly unfortunate background. Well, *she* didn't. No way. He'd loved every minute of his decadent existence with that crazy mother of his.

Yes, Nathan was as hard as nails and an opportunist of the first order, conning his way into her father's heart, getting Byron to adopt him, securing a cushy lifestyle and a fantastic job that he wouldn't have had a hope of winning with his pathetic education. People said he was clever and perhaps he was—not many people could whip off an award-winning play every year in their spare time—but he didn't even have his HSC, let alone a university degree, which was what her father had said *she* had to have before she was allowed to set one foot inside Whitmore Opals.

Nathan's cleverness, for want of a better word, lay in his ability to psychoanalyse people and play on their weaknesses.

From the word go, poor Byron had believed Nathan had turned over a new leaf where his morals were concerned. Pity her father hadn't kept his eyes open to what had happened around his own home from the moment he brought that walking phallic symbol into Belleview all those years ago.

But Byron hadn't, perhaps because he'd rarely been home himself. The head of Whitmore Opals was a workaholic of the worst kind, meaning well, but invariably neglectful of his family except in short bossy bursts. He was also totally ignorant of their true feelings and real natures. Even when it came to Nathan's marriage, Byron had a tendency to blame Lenore for everything from its shotgun beginning to its inevitable demise. As if any woman other than the most martyrish could endure marriage to a machine. Yes, Byron was blind to the real Nathan.

But that was understandable. Nathan could make others believe he was something he wasn't if it meant achieving one of his selfish ends. Look at how she'd adored him for years. Hero-worshipped him. Loved him.

She'd thought he'd at least liked her back. What he'd liked was wallowing in her unthreatening adoration, the adoration of a little girl. Now that she was a woman, with a woman's needs and desires, he'd turned on her. Not because he didn't desire her. She knew he did. My God, he'd had to scrape up every ounce of that amazing will-power of his to stop making love to her that afternoon a few months ago. But he'd managed, because an affair with her would have endangered what he desired more: Whitmore Opals. The Whitmore fortune.

With Jade being Byron's only natural-born child and a female to boot, Nathan probably figured he had a good chance of inheriting at least control of Whitmore's. Byron was a chauvinist of the first order who believed a woman's place was in the home, most certainly *not* in the boardroom of a company! His tirades against women like Celeste Campbell were never-ending.

Jade secretly admired the female head of Campbell Jewels. The woman was bold and beautiful, and more than a little brazen in the way she conducted her private life. But so what? If she'd been a man, there wouldn't be a whimper of protest or criticism. Alas, however, Celeste was a woman, and the old double standards applied. Her usually younger lovers were denigrated as toy-boys. She was slyly called a slut.

Which was what Nathan had said *she* was in danger of becoming, Jade recalled with a twisting inside. Now that was the pot calling the kettle black in her opinion! And not true, either. She could count her so-called lovers on one hand, and still have enough fingers left over to play 'Chopsticks'!

An angry indignation had her grabbing a towel from the nearby rail. But when she started vigorously rubbing herself dry, her bruised breasts moaned a protest. Looking down at them again, she suddenly burst into tears.

It took quite a while before Jade felt sufficiently in control to leave the sanctuary of her bedroom and face her family.

The house seemed unnaturally quiet as she made her way slowly down the huge sweeping staircase. Where was everyone? Sighing, she headed for the kitchen and laundry wing, where Melanie was sure to be located.

Jade was right. Belleview's highly efficient house-keeper was filling the dishwasher, looking her usual stark self, and quite out of place in the newly renovated all-white kitchen with its bright shiny surfaces. One could well imagine Melanie, with her solemn Madonna face, prim black top-knot and severe black dress, as the housekeeper in a Gothic novel, gliding silently through dimly lit rooms, the only lights in those dead black eyes of hers the flickering reflection of the candle she was holding.

Jade gave a little shiver at this highly evocative and almost frightening scenario.

Melanie straightened, turned and saw her. 'Hello, Jade,' the housekeeper greeted her in that expressionless voice of hers. 'I put your car around in the garages for you. You seemed to have a little trouble finding them last night,' she finished drily.

'What? Oh . . . oh, yes. Thanks, I was a little—er . . .'

'Blind?' Melanie suggested.

Jade laughed. If there was one thing she could count on at home, it was everyone's bad opinion. There would be no sympathy here, no understanding. Her reputation was totally shot around Belleview. What would be the point in telling Melanie that the sight of home with its solid safe walls had flooded her eyes with tears last night, making her run off the circular driveway, across the front lawn and into the cement surrounds of the large, lily-filled pond? Or that, still terribly shaken from her ordeal, she'd left her car there and staggered inside, taken more sleeping tablets than was good for her and crashed into blessed oblivion?

'Will you be staying for dinner tonight?' the house-keeper asked.

'If it's all right with you.' She was hoping to inveigle Nathan into going back with her to her unit tomorrow to see if Roberto and co were still there. Big brothers—even adopted ones who despised you—had to be good for something.

Melanie shrugged. 'Whatever. I have tomorrow off, though. You'll have to do for yourself or get Ava to cook for you.'

'Good God, no. Auntie's cooking is even worse than her watercolours. I'll rustle something up myself. Where is the old dear, by the way? And everyone else, for that matter? This place is like a morgue today.'

The housekeeper looked up with those dull black eyes of hers, giving Jade a droll glance before turning away to start loading the dishwasher. The clock on the oven said two-fifty, Jade noticed. The sleeping tablets had knocked her out for nearly twelve hours.

'Nathan's not here, if that's who you've come looking for,' Melanie informed her. 'He's taken Kirsty and Gemma with him to the beach-house at Avoca for the weekend.'

'Gemma?' The name was vaguely familiar but she couldn't place it. 'Who's Gemma?' Jade asked, ignoring Melanie's assumption she'd come visiting just to see Nathan.

'Kirsty's minder. Kirsty's living here for a while.'

'Oh? Why's that? Lenore found herself a lover at last?'

Jade suspected that after twelve years married to Nathan Lenore might find it hard to replace her husband with another man. From what she'd heard—and her own limited experience with him—the man was dynamite in bed.

'I have no idea what Lenore's private life is like,' Melanie said with cool rebuke in her voice. 'She was simply fed up with Kirsty's behaviour and thought a few weeks with her father might do her good. But with Nathan working late at Whitmore's every day, he felt he had to hire someone to personally supervise Kirsty before and after school.'

Jade laughed. 'I'll bet Kirsty just loves having a minder at fourteen.' Suddenly, the penny dropped on where she'd heard that name. 'This Gemma person wouldn't happen to be a lush young thing with big brown eyes, would she?'

Melanie's eyes snapped round, confirming Jade's intuitive guess.

'I happened to drop by a couple of weeks back,' Jade elaborated wryly. 'Nathan was just getting out of his car with the aforesaid nymph sitting in the passenger seat, looking as if butter wouldn't melt in her mouth. Nathan was doing a good imitation of a protective father figure but he didn't fool me for a second. I take it she's living in?'

Melanie nodded, and so did Jade. Slowly. Cynically.

'I'll bet she's not the same innocent young thing today that she was a couple of weeks ago.'

'I wouldn't bet too heavily on that,' Melanie said. 'Gemma's a strong-minded young woman with a wealth of character.'

'She'll need to be,' Jade muttered, surprised by Melanie's defence of this Gemma. *And* her confidence in the girl's will-power. Despite her deadpan exterior, Melanie was still a woman. She couldn't be ignorant of the magnetism of Nathan's sex appeal, even if only as an observer. The answer to the housekeeper's high opinion of the girl had to lie in the girl herself.

'So tell me about her,' Jade resumed, her curiosity piqued. 'Where did Nathan come across this gem of a Gemma?'

Melanie looked up. 'Careful...your claws are showing.'

Jade laughed, recognising the truth of this statement. Her feelings for Nathan perhaps weren't as vanquished as she'd thought they were.

'OK, OK,' she agreed. 'I sound like a jealous cat. So where does she come from?'

'Lightning Ridge.'

'The opal town way out back of Bourke?'

'That's the one. Nathan was out there buying opals for Byron and Gemma sold him some. It seems her father had just been accidentally killed—fell down a mine shaft—and she was selling up everything to come to Sydney. Nathan made her the offer of a job if she ever needed one.'

'Which she took him up on, of course,' Jade said ruefully. 'What girl wouldn't, after meeting Nathan? Say no more, I get the picture entirely.'

The housekeeper's sigh sounded exasperated.

'You can sigh, Melanie, but I saw the way that girl looked at Nathan the other week. Are you telling me she's *not* smitten by our resident Casanova?'

'All I'm saying is that she's not a pushover.'

'Meaning I am?'

Melanie gave her a sharp look. 'Don't go putting words into my mouth, Jade. You know better than anyone what sort of girl you are. I wouldn't dream of making such a judgement. I've only known you two years, six months of which you haven't even been living in this house. You weren't home much, even when you *were* living here.'

Jade's laugh was wry. 'I don't need to live here in person for you to have found out all the dirt on me. My mother used to adore telling everyone how bad I was. And it's all true. The climbing out of windows to meet boys in the middle of the night when I was only fifteen. Everything! I'm a bad 'un, Melanie. No doubt about it.'

'You and I both know you're not nearly as bad as you pretend to be, Jade,' Melanie astonished her by saying. 'Your teenage rebellions were revenge on your parents for their supposed lack of love, as well as some other imagined—or even real—transgressions.'

'My,' Jade returned caustically, 'What are you? The resident psychoanalyst around here?'

'I've had my share of experience with analysis,' Melanie said with not a flicker of retaliatory emotion.

Sympathy for this sad, soul-dead creature replaced Jade's anger. She knew about Melanie's past, how her husband and baby son had been killed in a car accident right before her eyes. It had been a horrific tragedy.

Yet while Jade could appreciate the numbing effect that would have on any wife and mother, it had been years now, for heaven's sake. Time to live again. Either that or put yourself out of your misery and throw yourself off a cliff or something.

Jade knew she herself would never commit suicide. She refused to let life get her *that* down. Life was meant to be lived, and, goddammit, she was going to live hers. To hell with her father, and Nathan, and even what had happened last night. And to hell with her mother. Irene was already probably in hell, anyway!

'Are you all right, Jade?' Melanie asked.

'Yes, of course.' She blinked rapidly, then tossed her head in memory of when her hair had recently been long and brown. After Nathan's rejection she had gone out and had most of her hair cut off, the remainder dyed whipped-cream blonde, shaved at the sides and spiked on top. Oddly, the outrageous style and colour suited her. Men now pursued her even more than they had before. 'I'm fine,' she lied blithely.

'You don't look fine. You look terrible.'

'Oh, that's just because of the sleeping tablets I took last night. They always leave me dopey the next day.'

'You shouldn't be taking sleeping tablets,' Melanie reproached seriously. 'You shouldn't even have them in your possession. They're like having a loaded gun around. People say they never mean to shoot anyone but if they didn't own a gun they couldn't. Same thing with sleeping tablets.'

Jade stared at the housekeeper, and wondered if she had once overdosed on sleeping tablets. Unexpectedly, Jade felt the urge to try to make friends with this woman whom she'd always pitied but never really liked. Now, she wanted to extend the hand of friendship, to see if she could help her in some way. But what to say, how to start? They were hardly of the same generation. Melanie had to be over thirty. If not, she sure looked it!

'Let's not talk of nasties,' Jade started up in her best breezy voice. 'How's things going with Auntie Ava? I presume she's up in that studio of hers, fantasising about Prince Charming sweeping into her life on a white charger. Has she finished any of those infernal paintings of hers, yet?'

'I would have thought your first concern would be your father, Jade, not your aunt.'

'I said no nasties, remember. Hopefully, Pops will stay put in that hospital a while longer. I can just about tolerate visiting him there. It's rather amusing seeing him trussed up in that pristine white bed with his leg in a sling. Of course, I haven't seen him for over a fortnight. We had the most frightful row over my appearance and that was that. What's he done? Has he been a bad boy? Banged up his leg again trying to seduce one of the nurses? He certainly wouldn't have tried it on the matron. What a tartar that woman is!'

Melanie smiled at Jade's ravings, shocking Jade. Why, the woman was quite striking when she smiled, with dazzling white teeth and eyes like glittering jet jewels. Not only striking, but sensual. The mock scenario of Byron trying to seduce the nurses seemed to have tickled the housekeeper's fancy, lending a decidedly sexy flavour to her smile.

Now Jade was floored. Melanie... *Sexy*? The idea was preposterous. And yet...

Jade looked at the housekeeper, really looked at her, mentally stripping away that shapeless black dress, trying to see the real woman behind the sexless façade. Her slender shoulders were broad, her breasts full, her waist and hips trim. And when she bent down over the dishwasher, her buttocks showed shapely and firm through the black gabardine. Her knees—what Jade could see of them—were very nice indeed. As were her ankles. Those ghastly thick beige stockings distracted from, but not entirely hid, the slender coltish lines of the legs inside them.

Jade tried to imagine what Melanie would look like in a slinky black dress, scarlet gloss on that sultry mouth of hers and sexy earrings swinging around that long white neck she had. Everyone's eyes round Belleview would fall right out of their sockets, her father included. He wouldn't recognise his prim and proper housekeeper.

A sudden memory stabbed at Jade's heart before the corner of her mouth lifted in a cynical smirk. It was just as well, perhaps, that Melanie was as she was, considering what had happened between the last housekeeper and the master of Belleview. Catching her father with that woman in his arms had come as a dreadful shock to Jade. Her god of a father, high on his pedestal—or was it podium?—always preaching about character and control and moral standards. Her father, having an affair with his housekeeper while his manic depressive wife was safely installed in a sanatorium somewhere.

He'd tried to explain everything away, saying he hadn't actually slept with the woman, saying he'd kissed her in a moment of weakness. Jade had not accused. She'd simply stood there, not listening, refusing to understand, unable to forgive, regardless of the circumstances. She couldn't abide parents who had the policy of 'don't do as I do, do as I say.'

She'd been just twenty at the time. Her father had dismissed the unfortunate woman—another injustice, she believed—and hired Melanie. But Jade had never looked at her father in the same way again. Neither had she taken a blind bit of notice of anything he tried to tell her. She went her own way, did her own thing. She had her own code of right and wrong, and had never hurt anyone as she was sure *he* had. He, *and* Nathan. *They* were the hurters, the despoilers.

Jade frowned as her mind shifted uncomfortably to her mother.

No, she decided abruptly. I will not make excuses. For either of them. For *any* of them!

An alien tap-tapping sound click-clacked somewhere in the house. Not recognising it, Jade swivelled on the kitchen stool she was perched up on, only to see her father making his way across the family-room, a walking cane in his right hand.

Their eyes met simultaneously through the open doorway, Jade's widening as Byron's narrowed. He looked hopping mad.

'You didn't give me a chance to tell you,' Melanie said quietly from the other side of the breakfast bar. 'Your father came home from the hospital yesterday.'

CHAPTER TWO

'YOU'VE changed your mind, it seems, about darkening this doorstep again,' Byron barked at his daughter.

'And hi to you, Pops,' Jade said with a flipness she fell into when at her most stressed. What on earth was her father doing home from hospital? A fortnight ago they'd said his leg wasn't mending properly and he'd be stuck in there for another month at least. She should have known he'd prove them wrong. 'You thinking of auditioning for the part of Long John Silver?' she quipped airily, waving at the walking cane.

Byron hobbled into the kitchen, still scowling at his daughter. 'One day you'll use that sassy mouth of yours on the wrong person. I hope I'm around to see it. Melanie, I'm expecting a visitor shortly. A Mr Armstrong. Show him into my study when he arrives, will you? And we'll be wanting coffee. Or tea, if he prefers. Ask him.'

'Certainly, Bryon. Will this Mr Armstrong be staying to dinner?'

'Maybe. Maybe not. I'll have to let you know.'

'And who is Mr Armstrong?' Jade asked, the name not at all familiar.

Byron's hard blue eyes swung back to his daughter. 'No one you know.' He looked her up and down, his upper lip curling with disgust at her appearance. 'Good God, girl, don't you ever wear a bra?' And, spinning round on his good leg, he limped off.

She pulled a face at his disappearing back. She *did* wear a bra... once every hundred years or so.

Admittedly, the ribbed pink vest-top she was wearing moulded her well-rounded breasts like a second skin, her nipples outlined and emphasised. But she hadn't brought any clothes with her and all that was in her wardrobe were things she hadn't worn for years, most of which were a little tight on her. She'd gone through a semi-anorexic stage back in her teens, till the loss of half her boobs had brought her up with a jolt. Horrified, she'd quickly eaten up till she was back to her shapely self, substituting the dieting with aerobics and weight-training. Her figure had steadily gone from gaunt to good to great. She was quite proud of it and had no intention of hiding her hard-earned shape under dowdy matronly clothes. Lord, she was only twenty-two, not fifty-two!

Sliding from the kitchen stool, however, reminded her that the jeans she had on were close to obscene, they were so tight. Maybe she should hunt out something of Auntie Ava's to put on. The old dear was always buying things in sales that were several sizes too small.

Jade was on the way through the family-room, heading in the direction of the front hall when the doorbell rang. 'I'll get it, Melanie,' she shouted back over her shoulder. 'It's sure to be the mysterious Mr Armstrong.'

'Find out if he's staying to dinner, will you, Jade?' Melanie called back. 'And if he wants tea or coffee.'

'Will do.'

She was whistling when she opened the door, her whistle changing to a low wolf-whistle as she took in the man standing there. God, but he was gorgeous! Tall, without being too tall, black curly hair, olive skin, lean saturnine features and piercing black eyes. His thick dark eyelashes were curly too, the bottom ones resting on high cheekbones that looked as if they'd been carved in stone.

He looked as if he'd been carved in stone, so still was he. And so totally unaffected by her none too subtle whistle.

Jade thought she detected the slightest flicker of something when his hard gaze raked over her eye-catching form. But if he was in any way impressed by what he saw he certainly didn't show it. Instead, there was a fractional lifting of his already sardonically arched eyebrows before he spoke in a voice reminiscent of Melanie's for its lack of emotion.

'Good afternoon,' he said coolly. 'Mr Whitmore is expecting me. Kyle Armstrong.'

I wonder if there's a *Mrs* Armstrong, was Jade's first thought, not at all put out by the man's apparent indifference to her charms. Nothing like a good challenge. It would make for a pleasant change. But she never tampered with married men. That was one of the lines she drew.

Pity other people didn't, she thought bitterly.

Her attention returned to the man before her. He wasn't wearing a wedding-ring but he was too good-looking not to be married. Taking a wild stab at his age, she came up with somewhere between twenty-eight and thirty-two. She was always hopeless at ages. She'd thought Roberto around thirty and he'd been closer to forty!

'Good afternoon, Mr Armstrong,' she greeted, holding out her hand and flashing him one of her most winning smiles. Her dentist had every reason to be proud of the perfectly even white teeth she displayed. 'Yes, my father mentioned he was expecting you. Do come in. I'll take you to him.'

Her smile turned slightly smug at Mr Armstrong's startled reaction to her announcing her relationship with the man he'd come to see. Possibly, he expected any daughter of the wealthy Byron Whitmore to be dressed a little more classily. Or maybe he hadn't known Byron *had* a daughter?

Now that was an interesting speculation. Still, Jade appreciated her father wouldn't go round proudly showing her photograph to every Tom, Dick and Harry. He was probably terrified one of them might recognise her as the little bit of fluff they'd had one night. After all, if she'd slept with as many men as her father and Nathan presumed, Byron was bound to come across one sooner or later!

Jade brushed aside the jab of dismay this thinking brought and wondered for the first time what business the gorgeous Mr Armstrong was in. He had to be calling on business. Why else would he be dressed in a dark grey suit on a hot Saturday afternoon? Besides, her father was not one for male friends of the personal kind. He *was* close to Nathan, and had a type of friendship with Zachary Marsden. But that too was partly business. Zachary had been the Whitmores' legal advisor for as long as she could remember.

Jade shut the front door and turned to their guest. He was no longer looking at her but was glancing around the house. Assessingly, she thought.

'This way...' She waved him along the downstairs hall that went under the staircase. Byron's study being the second last door on the right. 'Mr. Armstrong...' She began as they walked side by side.

'Kyle,' he returned coolly. 'Call me Kyle.'

'How nice. Kyle, then.' She smiled over at him. 'And I'm Jade.'

'Jade,' he repeated, but said nothing more. He didn't smile back, either.

Jade felt a momentary irritation. She didn't like men she couldn't read, or who didn't react the way she expected them to. It came to her abruptly that she didn't like men who were challenges after all. She much preferred men who fell victim to her charms immediately, and who pursued her doggedly. She enjoyed leading them a merry dance, making them almost beg for her favours, favours she did *not* bestow left, right and centre, *au contraire* to popular opinion.

She slid a sidewards glance over at the man beside her. In profile, he was not as pretty. His nose was sharp. His chin jutted stubbornly. He was not a man to beg for anything, of that she was certain. He was also staring steadfastly forward as they walked along the hallway together.

But if Jade's mind found Mr Armstrong's rude indifference highly offputting, her body did not. Just looking at him was making her stomach curl with a quite alien sensation. Dear God, but she would give anything to have him want her as she was suddenly wanting him.

Jade only managed to stop herself gasping in shock. For she had never really wanted a man like that in her entire life!

Oh, yes, she'd once been mad about the opposite sex, thriving on the dizzying excitement of being desired and needed and loved. But she'd been very young then, a teenager desperately looking for love and attention and approval, finding substitutes for all three in the kisses and arms of her boyfriends.

But she'd only had two actual lovers during her teenage years, not a zillion, her last serious relationship breaking up well before Nathan came back to Belleview to live after his separation from Lenore. That was when Jade's hero worship for her adopted brother had flared to a full-blown infatuation, and, while her feelings for Nathan had seemed part sexual at the time, she could see now that they hadn't touched the surface of real desire. Real desire was what she was feeling at this moment.

Yes, she'd tried to seduce Nathan, but not looking for sexual satisfaction—frankly, she'd never found intercourse at all memorable—but as a way to recapture his love and attention, the love and attention he'd once bestowed on her as a child and which had made her young life bearable. Admittedly, after that first bold kiss of hers, he'd quickly turned the tables on her, taking the initiative and managing to arouse her quite stunningly before he'd abruptly terminated the encounter. Her body had undoubtedly been left aching with physical frustration, which might explain why she'd raced precipitately into the arms of a new admirer a couple of days later.

The next morning, however, she'd felt ashamed of herself for the first time in her life. She'd only met the man the previous night at a party, where admittedly she'd had too much to drink. Not that that was any excuse. At least, she hadn't gone out with him again.

There had been several admirers since. But none had persuaded her into his bed.

Jade conceded, however, that Kyle Armstrong would not have much trouble doing just that.

Suddenly, she hoped he was married. That would put an end to this amazingly intense desire he'd somehow managed to spark in her. Her whole body felt tense and tingling by the time she stopped outside the study door and knocked.

'Yes,' boomed her father.

Opening the door, she popped her head inside. 'Mr Armstrong is here.'

'Well, bring him in, girl. Don't stand there looking ridiculous.'

Gritting her teeth, Jade threw open the door and waved their visitor inside.

He went, not giving her a second look. She was disgusted to find her heart was still racing and that her eyes were clinging to the back of that dark grey suit, to the way it fitted his nicely shaped shoulders like a glove. Jade had been on the end of undressing eyes from men before, but she'd never been guilty of doing such a thing herself. She was very definitely undressing Kyle Armstrong in her mind at that moment, however, and the results were unnerving. How was he managing to exude such a potent sexuality without even trying?

'Don't get up, Mr Whitmore,' Kyle said when Byron started struggling to his feet behind the huge desk. Striding over, he outstretched his long arm to shake Byron's hand. 'I'm so glad to meet you at last, sir. Talking on the telephone is not the same, is it?'

Jade saw her father look his guest up and down. Clearly, he liked what he saw almost as much as she did.

'It certainly isn't, my boy,' he said.

Jade dropped his age down to twenty-six or -seven. Her father would not call a man close to thirty...my boy.

'You were just leaving, Jade?' Byron snapped, making her seethe inside. How dared he dismiss her so rudely?

She delivered a saccharine smile his way. 'Melanie asked me to ask if Kyle was staying for dinner. Also, if he preferred tea or coffee.'

'You *know* Kyle here?' Byron ground out.

'Not till a minute ago,' she replied sweetly. And make of that what you will, you horny old hypocrite.

'Ah...'

His obvious relief infuriated the life out of her. 'Well?' she said sharply.

'What about it, Kyle? Can you stay for dinner? I'd like you to. I doubt if we'll have finished our discussions till then.'

'I'd love to stay,' he replied politely, still not looking at Jade. Suddenly, she felt like slapping his coolly supercilious face. Though poisoning would be better. She might slip some hemlock in his wine tonight.

But then she thought of a better vengeance for this snooty pair. Her father wanted her to wear a bra. Well, she would! At dinner tonight. A quite spectacular bejewelled corselette number that she'd bought for a fancy-dress costume a few years back and which would undoubtedly be at least one size too small. By God, if those unflappable dark eyes didn't fall out of their sockets when she walked into the dining-room wearing *that*, then she wasn't the girl voted most likely not to be a virgin in her last year at St Brigit's girls school.

'Tea or coffee?' she asked with the simpering sweetness of a Southern belle, fluttering her eyelashes when Kyle turned to glance her way at last.

'Coffee. Black, no sugar.'

Not a twitch. Not a flicker, either of irritation or amusement or anything. The man was a robot, she decided. A cold lifeless sexless robot. How could she have possibly thought he was sexy a moment ago?

But he was, she groaned silently. He most definitely was. God!

It struck Jade quite forcibly then that he couldn't be married. Married men always showed interest in her. *Always.*

She stared at him for a long moment with angry eyes, then, whirling, left the room, slamming the door behind her. 'Pompous fool!' she muttered aloud. 'Arrogant bastard,' she amended as she marched along the hallway.

By the time she reached the kitchen, various other unprintable descriptions had found favour, the last one bringing Melanie's eyes snapping up with startled surprise.

'Goodness! Who are you referring to? Surely not your father!'

'No. Kyle Armstrong. Mr. Cool-as-a-cucumber.'

'Oh, I see. You found him attractive and he didn't respond accordingly.'

When Jade glared outrage at Melanie, the housekeeper actually laughed. Once again, Jade was struck by the transformation in the woman once she abandoned her icy façade. What Melanie needed to snap her out of the past was some man to come along who could make her smile and laugh again. Laughter made life bearable.

Jade wagged a finger at Melanie. 'I haven't given up yet,' she warned. 'Mr Armstrong's staying for dinner.'

'Is he, now? And what are you going to do, come down to dinner in your birthday suit?'

'Not quite.'

'Has it ever occurred to you that some men just don't like women who are obvious in their pursuit of them?'

Jade declined telling Melanie that it didn't work if you dressed like a nun and acted like a corpse, either. 'I don't intend chasing the man. I simply want him to see what he could have if *he* chased *me*!'

'And what if he doesn't choose to chase you? What if he likes more subtle women whose clothing hints at their charms rather than shoves it in their faces?'

'I don't shove my charms in men's faces!' Jade protested.

'Don't you?' Melanie's eyes slid drily over the skin-tight jeans and top. 'Look, Jade, you can get away with things at university that the more mature world won't tolerate kindly. How old is this Mr Armstrong?'

Jade shrugged. 'Late twenties, I think. But he acts like he's pushing forty.'

Melanie smiled. 'In that case, if you want to attract his attention, perhaps you should adopt a more mature fashion sense and attitude.'

'I'd rather be dead than dress and act like some snobbish society bitch,' she pouted. 'They all look the same, as if they've been poured out of a mould. If Mr Kyle Armstrong doesn't like the way I am then he can drop dead. I won't play ice princess for any man.'

'Then you'd better resign yourself to losing out this time.'

'We'll see,' Jade bit out, and went to leave. 'Oh, by the way,' she added, stopping to look back over her shoulder. 'He likes coffee. Black, no sugar. Same as me.'

With that, she stalked from the kitchen, determined strides carrying her across the family-room to the front foyer, up the stairs two at a time and along the picture-lined gallery down to Ava's studio. Bursting in without knocking, she threw a greeting at her startled aunt before plonking herself down on the much used divan. With a disgruntled sigh, she rearranged the many pillows and lay down, stretching out her long legs.

'I've had it with Pops, Auntie,' she grumbled. 'Really had it!'

'Tell me something new, Jade, dear.' Ava put down her paintbrush and wandered over to stare down at her niece. She took one look at the dark smudges under the girl's eyes and felt a surge of sympathy. She'd always liked Jade, felt the girl had got a raw deal in life with Irene as a mother and Byron as a father. Things hadn't improved much with Byron bringing Nathan home, either. Having someone like Nathan as an adopted brother was no help at all. Ava had been relieved when Jade finally left home. Nothing like having to do for oneself to make one grow up, and grow.

Ava silently wished she had the courage to buck her big brother's controlling hand and do the same. But it was too late for her. Far too late...

'At least you don't have to stay, if your father annoys you, dear. Why are you here, by the way? Melanie told me at breakfast that you'd come home during the night.'

Ava was shocked by the haunted, almost horrified look that zoomed into her niece's dark blue eyes. But the fear vanished almost before Ava could be sure that was what she'd seen, replaced by one of Jade's nonchalant *c'est la vie* expressions. Ava had always admired the girl's courage and spirit, but it worried her that she buried far too many problems behind that good-time-girl persona. Clearly, something had happened last night to send Jade running for home like a frightened child. But she knew Jade too well to hope she'd confide in her stuffy old aunt.

'Oh, just thought I'd drop in and see how the old family was doing,' Jade said, waving an airy hand. 'I didn't know Pops was home, of course. Or that Nathan had escaped to Avoca with his daughter and his girlfriend.'

Ava frowned. '*Girlfriend*? Oh, you mean Gemma. She's not Nathan's girlfriend, Jade, she's—'

'Kirsty's minder,' Jade broke in drily. 'Yes, I gather that's the occupation she goes under. But you and I both know, Auntie, that she'll be providing some extra services before long.'

'I think that is Nathan and Gemma's business, don't you?' Ava rebuked gently. 'After all, Nathan's divorced and Gemma's single.'

'Single! She's barely out of nappies.'

'She's nearly twenty, Jade, only two years your junior. You didn't seem to think Nathan was too old for you a while back.'

'Auntie!' Jade mocked. 'Have you been spying on me?'

'One hardly needs to spy on you, Jade, dear. You flaunt your feelings for all to see. You flaunt your other attributes as well,' she added, casting an acerbic eye over the girl's eyecatching and obviously braless figure.

For once, her niece seemed bothered by criticism over her appearance. Normally, she responded by being even more outrageous.

Jade sat up, glancing down at her body with a frown on her face. 'Melanie was saying much of the same a minute ago,' she muttered unhappily. 'But honestly, Auntie, I don't like stuffy clothes. And I don't like stuffy people, especially stuffy men!'

Ava laughed. 'What man's been putting your nose out of joint?'

'Some nerd Pops is holed up with in his study. Do you know him? He goes by the name of Mr Kyle Armstrong.'

'Ah... the whizkid from Tasmania.'

'And?'

Ava walked back over to sit down at her easel. She picked up her paintbrush and started dabbing before she satisfied Jade's curiosity. 'Can't tell you much. He's a marketing expert your father is thinking of hiring to jazz up Whitmore Opals.'

'Jazz up? That man couldn't jazz up anything. If Pops wants someone to jazz up Whitmore Opals why doesn't he hire someone with a bit of flair, someone modern and really young? Someone like me! I'm specialising in marketing at uni this year. I'll have my degree in November. God, I don't believe this. I'm so mad I could spit.' She jumped to her feet and started pacing the room.

'One is hardly likely to hire an undergraduate for head of marketing, Jade,' her aunt advised logically.

But Jade didn't feel logical. Fury and resentment were firing her blood. Not only did she have Nathan coveting control of the entire Whitmore fortune—the family had fingers in many pies besides opals—now she had her father overlooking his own daughter to hire some pompous upstart into the very job she'd been going to invent herself after she'd gained her marketing degree. Up till this point, Whitmore Opals didn't even *have* a marketing section, let alone a head of it. Byron had been only too happy to be head of everything: managing, selling, marketing, buying, advertising.

Jade's temper was reaching boiling point when she suddenly realised this could be turned to her advantage. Why, if she played her cards right, she might be able to get the super-cool and undoubtedly ambitious Mr Armstrong on her side. By reminding him on the sly that

she was the boss's daughter and a marketing undergraduate, she might be able to con him into letting her
work part-time in the office, so gaining some valuable
training. Maybe once she showed her father she could
be as clever and competent as any man, he would relin-
quish that stupid old-fashioned idea that a woman had
no place in business.

Of course, to achieve such an end, she would have to
present a slightly more conservative image, as Melanie
had suggested. Any thought of wearing that ridiculously
provocative corselette would have to be abandoned. She
might even have to wear a *normal* bra.

'Auntie,' she said slowly, 'you wouldn't mind if I
looked through your wardrobe, would you? I might
borrow something for dinner tonight. Mr Armstrong is
dining with us.'

'I think you'll find it a bit depleted, dear. I gave
everything that didn't fit me to Gemma.'

Jade couldn't believe it. What kind of girl was this
Gemma person that everyone was so taken with her? No
doubt her own father thought she was just the ants'
pants, not like his own cheap, vulgar tramp of a daughter.
God, she hoped Nathan hurried up and corrupted that
girl. And she hoped everyone found out about it, including her father.

Grumbling under her breath, she decided there was
nothing else to do but go downstairs and throw herself
on Melanie's mercy. The woman had to have something
in her wardrobe besides those hideous black dresses she
always wore.

Before she left, she wandered over to look at her aunt's
painting.

'Hey,' she said, surprise in her voice. 'That's rather
good. You must be improving, Auntie.'

'Either that, or your taste is,' Ava countered with uncharacteristic wit. She and her niece exchanged startled
glances.

'Goodness, Auntie,' Jade laughed. 'That was quick.'

'Yes, it was, wasn't it?'

Jade gave her a considering look. 'You seem happier, do you know that?'

'You could be right. The whole house has been happier since Gemma came to live here.'

'God, not that girl again! I'll have to meet this paragon of perfection soon or I'll explode with envy and irritation!'

Now Ava laughed. 'She'll have you eating out of her hand in no time, just as she has everyone else.'

'I wouldn't bet on that if I were you, Auntie.' And, thinking darkly jealous thoughts, Jade marched from the room.

Gemma propped herself up on one elbow and looked down at the naked man sleeping beside her. He was so beautiful.

Her eyes caressed his perfect profile, his gorgeous golden hair, tousled at the moment, and that glorious mouth, full-lipped and sensual but not at all feminine. There wasn't a feminine bone in Nathan Whitmore's beautiful bronzed body.

Hard to believe he was thirty-five.

Hard to believe that less than an hour ago she had been a fear-filled, quivering virgin.

Hard to believe he wanted to marry *her*, a silly little country girl not yet twenty. She couldn't believe her luck.

'You're making me self-conscious, staring at me like that,' he murmured, his left eye flicking half open.

'Oh! I...I thought you'd fallen asleep.'

'Just resting,' he whispered, and reached for her.

Gemma gave herself up momentarily to the excitement of his kisses, but as soon as he lifted his mouth to take a breath, she wriggled out of his arms and away from further temptation.

'We have to stop, Nathan,' she said breathlessly. 'Kirsty might come back from the beach at any moment. She's been gone over an hour. It's nearly three.'

It was only by chance that Gemma wasn't down at the beach with Kirsty. But she hadn't liked the sea; hadn't liked it at all.

'Kirsty never leaves the beach till the sun goes down,' Nathan reassured her. 'Still, it's possible, I suppose, and I wouldn't want her to catch us together like this.' He trickled a hand over Gemma's breasts, smiling softly as an involuntary tremor rippled through her. 'My own lovely little Gemma,' he said, and bent to flick a moist fingertip over the nearest erect nipple. 'Do you realise we'll have all night together now that Kirsty's going to that movie marathon?'

Gemma tried to dampen down her excitement at such a prospect to focus on Nathan's daughter. 'I'm not sure Lenore would be happy with Kirsty going to an all-night movie session, Nathan. She's only fourteen, after all. Not only that, she's supposed to be grounded for another week.'

At the mention of his ex-wife, Nathan scowled and rolled away, planting angry feet on the floor beside the bed. 'I'll make the decisions for my daughter while she's under my roof. Lenore can go jump.'

Gemma was taken aback by Nathan's burst of temper, so unlike his usual cool self. Her mind flashed to that kiss she'd witnessed between him and his ex-wife less than two weeks before, on the very first night she'd come to Belleview. It had been one of the main reasons she'd fought her attraction for Nathan, thinking he was still in love with Lenore. The passion of the last hour had deflected her mind away from any earlier doubts, but now the possibility that the man she loved still harboured strong feelings for the woman he'd been married to for twelve years raised its ugly head again.

'She's Kirsty's mother,' Gemma argued unhappily. 'I think her feelings have to be considered.'

Nathan started pulling on his clothes, his actions jerky. 'As if that selfish bitch has got any real feelings,' he muttered.

Gemma stared at him. When Nathan saw her shocked expression he leant back over the bed to cup her chin and kiss her lightly on the mouth. 'Not like you, my darling girl. You have more feeling in your little finger than Lenore has in her whole body.'

Then why were you kissing her less than two weeks ago as if you wanted to devour her? she was dying to ask. Instead, she said tremulously, 'You do love me, don't you, Nathan?'

'*Love* you? I *adore* you.' His mouth returned to hers, demanding and hungry. He groaned and pushed her back on the pillows.

'Nathan, we can't!' she gasped.

'There's no such thing as can't, Gemma,' he growled. 'Only won't.' He buried his face between her breasts, then slowly slid downwards.

'You...you shouldn't,' she managed in a weak whisper, both embarrassed and fascinated by what he was now doing. For a while the embarrassment won, her face flaming, her hands fluttering helplessly by her sides. But then sheer physical pleasure triumphed over any shock or shame. Her fingers started grasping the sheets on either side of her, and her mind spun out into a void of endless delight.

CHAPTER THREE

JADE surveyed her reflection in the mirror with mischievous satisfaction. Melanie had come through with a navy linen suit that would have looked ghastly if Jade had worn the white silk blouse with the tie at the throat that went with it. Instead, she'd filled the deep V neckline with a lacy pink camisole rescued from the depths of Auntie Ava's wardrobe. The dear old thing had also produced a pair of dainty pink sandals with outrageously high heels, a relic from her partying days.

Digging deep in her own drawers, Jade had come up with some pink multi-disc earrings which she'd adored as a teenager but which hadn't seen the light of day since. Oddly enough, they looked very effective with her new short blonde hair.

The combination of the sedate and the saucy produced a highly tantalising whole, which hinted—as Melanie and Ava had suggested—but was still sexy at the same time. Of course, Jade couldn't resist the naughty little added touches, such as painting her toenails a vibrant pink, then leaving off tights. She'd also turned over the waistband of the knee-length pleated skirt a couple of times so that the hem swirled mid-thigh when she turned around. She made a mental note to turn around often.

Only once during her dressing did Jade's mind whip back to the distressing events of the previous evening. Melanie had lent her a bra—they were around the same size—but Jade found her bruised breasts too sore to tolerate the constriction. For a moment, as she was forced to face her physical damage, fear swept in again, but this was swiftly followed by a bitter fury. Being a quivering victim was not Jade's style. She gritted her teeth and vowed she would not let some pervert damage her mind. He could damage her body—that would heal!—

but not her mind. Her mind was her own. She refused to have it warped or twisted. If she did, she might end up like her mother. Now there was a warped and twisted mind if ever there was one!

So with her freshly shampooed and moussed hair teased to its maximum height on top of her head, and enough Spellbound perfume on to cast a thousand spells, Jade swanned downstairs and along to the formal drawing-room where Melanie said her father was having pre-dinner drinks with his guest. The grandfather clock in the hall donged seven-thirty as Jade passed. Dinner had been ordered for eight.

Both men were sitting down when she sashayed in, her father on the green velvet sofa that faced the fireplace, while Mr Cool occupied one of the overstuffed brocade armchairs that flanked the marble hearth. There were no guesses which one drew her attention first.

Hell, but he looked as lethally attractive sitting there, sipping his drink, as did the drink he was sipping. By the colour, it had to be straight Johnny Walker. Jade conceded she could have done with a stiff drink herself right at that moment, her courage in danger of failing her. What was it about this man that rattled her so— the fact that she fancied him so badly, or that *he* didn't fancy *her* at all?

She resisted licking suddenly dry lips and kept moving into the room, her skirt swishing around her bare legs, her eyes still on Kyle Armstrong, waiting for—no, hoping for—a favourable reaction to her vastly changed appearance.

His eyes lifted as she approached, locking with hers. They remained perfectly steady, showing nothing in their coal-black depths that she could read. But he didn't turn his eyes away and oddly she gained the impression he was challenging her, no, *compelling* her to keep looking at him. Suddenly she felt the power of his mental strength, and her knees almost went from under her. This most uncharacteristic weakness unnerved Jade, unnerved then annoyed her.

Gathering herself, she shot him a bold smile, hoping to ruffle his equilibrium as much as his gypsy-eyed stare had ruffled hers. But he didn't smile back, merely lifted his drink to his lips again, keeping up his cool assessment of her over the rim.

Jade found her smile fading and an amazing blush heating her cheeks. Totally rattled now, she wrenched her eyes away from him to land on her frowning father, who couldn't seem to make up his mind whether he liked how she looked or not. She appreciated his ambivalence, and found amusement in it, thank heavens. She needed *something* to break this awful tension that had been invading her since entering the room.

'Good evening, Father, dear,' she said, abandoning her usual address of Pops. 'Kyle,' she added, inclining her head their guest's way without actually meeting his eyes.

Both said good evening back as she continued over to the rosewood drinks cabinet, where she mixed herself a triple Scotch and ginger ale, taking a deep swallow before returning to make the twosome a far from cosy threesome.

Her father clicked his tongue impatiently when he had to move his cane for her to sit down next to him. 'Did you finish whatever it was you had to finish?' she enquired casually, crossing her legs and tucking her ankles back toward the base of the sofa.

'I think we tied up everything to our mutual satisfaction, wouldn't you say, Kyle?' Byron conceded, his reply not really telling her anything.

'Yes, indeed,' came Mr Cool's equally uninformative remark.

Piqued, Jade decided to put this chauvinistic pair on the spot. 'Auntie Ava says Kyle is going to be the new head of marketing at Whitmore Opals—is that right?'

'Damned woman,' Byron muttered under his breath.

Jade laughed. 'Did I hear right, Father, dear? Are you calling me a woman at last?'

His hard blue eyes turned her way. Clearly, he would have liked to tear strips off her for her impudence, but the presence of a guest stopped him. With a great effort of will, Byron relaxed back on the sofa and found a smile that should have warned her what was coming.

'A real woman is more than a set of curves, daughter, dear,' he said with poisonous pointedness.

'So true, so true,' she returned airily after taking another deep swallow of her drink. 'And a real man is more than an impressive set of—er—muscles. Don't you agree, Kyle?' she finished, flashing him a mock-innocent smile.

Good God, was she imagining things or was that actually a twinkle of amusement in those implacable dark eyes of his? His mouth, however, maintained its habitual straight line, though he did cover it slightly by lifting his drink to his lips once more.

The glass retreated and yes, his mouth was as unmoved as before. 'I most certainly do agree, Jade,' he said smoothly. 'And you're right about that other matter as well. Byron has offered me the position as marketing manager and I have accepted.'

Most Australians didn't move their lips much when they spoke. Kyle Armstrong, however, had a surprising mobile mouth when he talked, his voice clear, cultured and well enunciated, like an actor. It drew one's attention to his mouth, and his lips.

Intriguing lips, those, Jade realised, her gaze fastening on them, the top one thin and cruel, the bottom soft and sensual. Which was the real man? God, she just had to find out. But *how*? He wasn't at all impressed by her. Or interested.

Or was he?

Her eyes lifted to that enigmatic gaze of his, only to find it fixed on the expanse of tanned thigh she was showing. Jade's heart began to beat faster. Maybe he *was* a little interested. Maybe he was just good at hiding it. Maybe it was only her father's presence that stopped him from showing any interest. What was he wondering while he looked at her legs? Was he speculating what it might be like to get lost between them?

Jade found herself pressing her thighs tightly together, appalled by the escalating explicitness of her thoughts.

So this was lust, she thought dazedly.

This was one of the seven deadly sins.

No wonder people fell prey to its seductive power. She'd never felt so excited, so *driven*.

Once again, she started hoping that Kyle might be married, so that she had a good reason to fight this alien force that was possessing her.

'Are you married, Kyle?' she asked abruptly.

'No,' he said, his brows drawing slightly together as his eyes lifted to hers. 'Why do you ask?'

Perversely, she was relieved by the news, which didn't augur well for her future behaviour. Jade suspected she was about to embark on a course of action even more outrageous than any she'd ever been accused of. 'I was just wondering what your wife—if you had one,' she added with a husky laugh, 'might think of her husband moving interstate for a job.'

'How did you know that...?' The corner of his mouth tipped up into the tiniest of rueful smiles. 'Ah...your Auntie Ava again?' he suggested drily.

'Of course.'

'I'll never tell that infernal woman another damned thing!' Byron pronounced testily from the other end of the sofa.

'Poor Auntie,' Jade muttered before rounding on her father, her voice sharp. 'Why all the cloak and dagger stuff, anyway? Who'd care if Mr. C—?' She broke off, her eyes widening. My God, she'd almost called him Mr Cool out loud! Clearing her throat as a cover, she said 'excuse me', then sipped her drink. A fit of mad giggles sprang to her throat but she managed to stifle the urge and continue in a surprisingly normal voice. 'I was going to say why shouldn't other people know about Kyle's appointment?'

'Because I don't want Celeste Campbell to get wind of it, that's why!' Byron snarled.

Jade raised her eyebrows. She often wondered what had happened between her father and Celeste Campbell to make their relationship so vitriolic on his side, and continuingly vengeful on hers. Celeste was, in fact, Jade's aunt, being her mother's half-sister. Her mother, Irene, had been Stewart Campbell's first-born child, but his wife had passed away within weeks of Irene being born and the widower Campbell had subsequently remarried and had two more children, Celeste and Damian.

Jade found the antagonism between her father and Celeste Campbell quite perplexing. The ancient feud between their fathers, David Whitmore and Stewart Campbell, was well known, though not the reason behind it. Something to do with an opal, she had heard once, a very valuable one which had disappeared or something.

Whatever, after the two men passed away, her parents' marriage had seemed to heal the rift between the families to a degree. Enough, anyway, for the old animosity to die down to nothing but normal competition between business people who shared a common trade. Apparently, however, when Celeste had taken control of Campbell Jewels about ten years ago, she'd found cause to resurrect the old feud between the Campbells and Whitmores.

It was a mystery all right and one which she didn't think she'd ever solve. Her father was not about to confide in her. Neither was Celeste Campbell. Maybe they just hated each other's guts. Or, more likely, Jade's mother had stirred up some trouble. Irene had bad-mouthed Celeste every chance she got.

'I doubt Ms Campbell could do much more to Whitmore's than she's been doing,' Jade commented wryly.

'You don't give an enemy any advantage,' her father snapped.

'But *why* is she your enemy, Father? What did you do to her, or vice versa? I've always wanted to know.'

'I do not wish to discuss this topic at this juncture, thank you, Jade. Kyle doesn't want to hear our family dirty linen aired, I'm sure.'

Dirty linen? That sounded intensely personal and far darker than anything she'd been imagining.

Jade stared at her father for a second before recovering. 'I'm sure Kyle would like to be acquainted with the nature of the competition between Campbell's and Whitmore's. He needs to know what he's up against.'

'He already knows what he's up against. Celeste Campbell is a conniving, ambitious, vengeful bitch who will stop at nothing to ruin me. There's no more to be said!'

Melanie's entering the room at that precise moment to announce dinner was a frustration to Jade. For there was a lot more to be said. The frown on Kyle's face showed he agreed with her. Maybe he was even having second thoughts about the difficult job he was taking on. Jade suspected that if the family had had to rely on the profits from Whitmore Opals over the past few years they would be in deep financial straits. Fortunately, during the good years, both Grandfather Whitmore and her own father had diversified their investments into property and blue-chip stocks and shares.

Not that Jade had to rely on her family—or her father—for money any more. When she'd turned twenty-one last year, she'd inherited a substantial income from a trust her grandmother had set up for her before she was even born. This had been added to with her mother's recent estate, which included a lot of valuable jewellery.

Unhappy about taking anything from her mother, Jade had left the jewels to languish in the family safe. Thinking about them now, she decided she would give them all to Auntie Ava. The poor dear had to ask Byron for every single cent, her big brother having been made executor of her inheritance till she married, a most unsatisfactory arrangement for any self-respecting female. No wonder she buckled under his will all the time. She would advise Ava to sell some of the jewellery and do something with the proceeds. Go to a proper art school. Or take off on a world cruise. Who knew? Maybe she'd even meet her Prince Charming if she got out and about. And maybe she'd lose some weight!

'This way, Mr Armstrong,' Melanie was directing their guest in her cool, slightly imperious manner. 'I hope you like lamb...'

Jade was left to help her father struggle to his feet. 'Here, lean on me, Pops,' she offered.

'So it's "Pops" now, is it?' he frowned. 'What happened to "Father dear"? Or was that only to impress our visitor?'

'Naturally,' she grinned, and hoisted her father's arm around her shoulders. He grunted with real pain when his weight shifted across his bad leg.

'I'll bet you signed yourself out of that hospital too soon, didn't you?' Jade accused.

'Bloody hospitals should be banned. Torture chambers, all of them.'

Jade laughed.

'You have a nice laugh, daughter, do you know that?'

'*You* certainly haven't told me before. Watch the edge of that coffee-table!'

They watched it together as she manoeuvred Byron into clear territory. The drawing-room was rather cluttered with a myriad antiques and expensive knickknacks.

'You're strong, aren't you?' Byron commented with surprise in his voice. 'You have broad shoulders. Must take after your father.'

'Part of what you're feeling is shoulder pads,' she said, not sure how to take this shift in the conversation. If she didn't know better, she might think her father was trying to make up with her after their last row, not to mention his earlier rudeness.

'I can manage by myself now,' he said curtly, as though embarrassed by his conciliatory behaviour and taking it back. 'Hand me my cane.'

She did. Smiling.

He caught the smile and smiled back.

Jade's heart contracted. Why did she love him so much when he was such a cantankerous bastard, and when he lived his life by typically male standards? Did he honestly think she believed that one incident had been his one and only transgression with other women while her mother was alive? Good God, just look at him! Fifty years old with a bung leg and a scowling face and he'd still stop most women dead in their tracks at a single glance. His body was still hard, his head still full of hair. And those hard blue eyes were so damned sexy it was sinful.

'You're a good girl,' he said. 'Underneath. And you look very nice tonight.'

Jade's smile widened.

'What's the private joke?' he demanded to know.

'It was the underneath part. I still haven't got a bra on, you know.'

'No, I didn't know. And neither would any other man looking at you in that rig-out, which is exactly how it should be. The only man who should see a woman's bare breasts is her husband!'

'I'll keep that in mind, Pops.'

Jade resisted telling her father that the last thing she was ever going to have was a husband. Marriage, in her books, was not the key to eternal happiness. She couldn't deny men filled a necessary niche, every once in a while. But as a daily diet?

Good God, no. Marriage was not for her. No way. She did her own thing, ran her own race, thank you very much. Imagine being married to someone like Mr Cool. In no time, he would be telling her what to wear, how to act, how to *vote*, even! Men like him couldn't seem to help taking on the role of bossy-boots. The poor darlings actually thought they knew best, that the world would stop spinning if they didn't spin it personally.

No, she was not interested in marrying Kyle Armstrong. She simply wanted to sleep with him. There! She could admit it now and not tremble with shock. And if she could wangle a position for herself at Whitmore Opals at the same time, then so much the better!

The grandfather clock slowly and sombrely donged eight as they passed, as though giving her a grave warning about something. Jade ignored the omen. She didn't believe in such things.

* * *

Eight o'clock found Gemma finding a temporary sanctuary in the swimming-pool. She stroked up and down, up and down, wishing she could recapture the euphoria she'd felt earlier that afternoon in Nathan's arms. But reality had come back with a rush and it was impossible to stop all the doubts and fears from crowding her mind.

What was everyone in Belleview going to say when she and Nathan announced one day in the near future that they were married? Maybe Byron wouldn't be too surprised—she had an odd feeling he already knew there was something between herself and Nathan. Neither would Ava or Melanie be too shocked. But they wouldn't be at all pleased. They might start thinking she was a little schemer, that she'd inveigled her way into Belleview in order to entrap Nathan into marriage.

She could perhaps endure that. Kirsty's reaction, however, loomed as a major problem. Nathan's daughter was going to feel betrayed. Gemma had become the girl's friend, more than her minder. How was Kirsty going to react when she found out Gemma had married her father, the father she still hoped would be reconciled with her mother?

Gemma hated even thinking about it. She also hated having to pretend there was nothing between herself and Nathan till they were safely married. She'd always believed honesty was the best policy. Deception and lies were wrong.

But Nathan insisted they keep their relationship a secret till after the event. He wanted no fuss, he said. No arguments. People would try to talk them out of marrying if they knew beforehand.

Which people? she'd asked as soon as Kirsty had left the house to go to the movie marathon with her friends. Was he talking about Byron? Ava? His daughter? His ex-wife? Was it *himself* he feared could be talked out of the marriage. Or *herself*?

Nathan hadn't really answered her. He'd diverted her questions by making love to her yet again. Afterwards, while he was in the bathroom, she'd slipped on her swimming costume and fled to the pool, anywhere where she could think. The suspicion that Nathan might deliberately have used sex to silence her arguments was now teasing the edges of her mind, and, while she automatically shrank from the idea, Gemma found it wouldn't let go. If anything, it was growing.

A splash behind her had her feet searching for the bottom of the pool. But she was at the deep end, so she was madly treading water when Nathan swam underneath her feet and surfaced in front of her.

'I couldn't find you,' he said, slicking his hair back from his handsome but angry eyes. 'Why didn't you tell me where you were going? I wouldn't have known where you were if I hadn't looked out of the study window.'

'I...I needed some air,' she answered breathlessly, already feeling tired. She wasn't the strongest swimmer in the world. If there hadn't been a learn-to-swim programme at school she never would have learnt at all. Lightning Ridge did not abound in water.

'Have you changed your mind?' he asked coldly. 'About getting married.'

'No, of course not. It's just that it isn't going to be easy. I...I'm worried about what Kirsty's going to say.'

'Kirsty will adjust. So will everyone else. Just do as I say and everything will be fine. Here, you're sinking. Put your arms around my neck and wrap your legs around my waist.'

She went to do so but jerked back as though stung. 'You're...you're naked!'

'Uh-huh. And so will you be...once I get you out of this strait-jacket.'

Gemma gasped as her breasts burst free of her costume, Nathan peeling the purple maillot downwards till it was dragged right off and let go of, to float away. For a while she trod water again, her flapping arms and legs making her even more aware of her abrupt nudity. She glanced nervously around, happy to see that the trees and shrubbery around the edges of the garden gave them privacy from neighbors. The sun had not long set but the evening was warm. Stars twinkled overhead in a clear sky. A half-moon bathed the water in its soft glow.

'I ... I'm not used to this kind of thing,' she babbled.

'I know,' he said, and caught her to him.

His mouth was wet and warm and wild. Gemma wanted to push him away, to say she had things she needed to talk about, but she soon ran up the white flag. Making love with the man she loved was too new and too wonderful and too exciting to replace with serious discussion. That could wait, she supposed. After all, they did have all night.

With a sigh, she moved to fit her body to his, to entwine her arms and legs around his hard lean torso. Nathan groaned deep in his throat and clasped her even closer. Gemma's head whirled and she pushed all thought of Kirsty aside. It was a night made for love, a night made for lovers. She would worry about tomorrow ... tomorrow.

CHAPTER FOUR

JADE watched Melanie steering their dinner guest into the dining-room ahead of them, her conversation obviously finding favour with Mr Cool, since he was smiling over at the housekeeper. A pang of jealousy was quickly followed by a surge of annoyance. What was wrong with her today, becoming fixated on a man who obviously did not return her interest? A challenge was all very well but when it started affecting her total equilibrium then it was time to call a halt!

Besides, she couldn't possibly be wanting Kyle as much as she thought she did. Sex for sex's sake had never held any fascination for her. How could it when the physical act left her unmoved? It was male attention she occasionally craved, not male bodies.

Nathan was the only man ever to have really aroused her. But then Nathan was an enigma in that regard. Men like him should be banned from female company. They were far too dangerous.

As for men like Mr Cool... Jade was at a loss to understand why she was finding him so physically fascinating. One would think that after last night her susceptibility to the male sex would have to be at an all-time low. Yet here she was, being plagued by feelings she didn't want, and desires that were so alien to her that she didn't really know how to handle them.

Feeling irritated and somewhat bewildered, Jade fell uncharacteristically silent. Too bad her father wasn't similarly content.

'Well, what do you think of him?' he demanded to know as they made slow progress together towards the dining-room.

Jade suppressed a sigh. 'I think I'll reserve judgement for now.'

48

He threw her a knowing look. 'You don't like him.'

'I didn't say that.'

'You don't have to. I picked up your vibes back in the drawing-room.'

Jade was astonished. If there'd been any vibes to pick up, they certainly weren't dislike. Or were they? Maybe she would instinctively dislike any man who endangered her need always to be in control of her life, regardless of whatever other feelings he evoked in her. And Kyle Armstrong was doing that. Somehow...

'What do you know about him?' she asked.

'Enough.'

'How did you find him?'

'Through one of those head-hunter agencies. His credentials are second to none.'

'Naturally,' she muttered.

They turned into the dining-room, where their guest was already seated next to a pink-faced Ava, who was never at her best with strangers. Still, this particular stranger was apparently being as charming to her as he had been with Melanie, Jade noted tartly, since her aunt was smiling prettily at him.

'So there you are, Ava,' Byron roared. 'I've got a bone to pick with you!'

Jade was furious with her father for hollering at his poor sister like that and making her jump nervously in her seat. To give him credit, Kyle didn't look all that impressed with Byron either, though he was quick to hide his annoyance. Jade didn't feel at all disposed to hide her own irritation.

'Don't be such a bully, Pops. Auntie, take no notice of him. He's out of sorts because his leg hurts and he's got no one left to boss around, now that I've left the nest. One would think he'd be on his best behaviour with a guest in the house.' This with a sardonic lifting of eyebrows Kyle's way. 'But of course, wealthy men don't bow to such niceties. They forge on regardless, being rude and trying to intimidate everyone around them.'

Jade was startled to note Kyle looking at her with an expression akin to admiration in his eyes. Admiration, and something else. Was it amusement at last? Hard to tell behind that inscrutable face of his. Whatever, it egged her on to more outrageousness.

'Money and manners don't often mix, I've found,' she continued, a saucy smile teasing her wide, pink-glossed mouth. 'Sit down, Pops, and I'll put some mood music on.'

'None of that modern garbage,' Byron muttered, though doing his daughter's bidding and sitting down meekly enough.

'I'll bet that's just what Beethoven's father said when his son produced his latest symphony,' Jade quipped. 'What kind of music do you like, Kyle?' she asked, sending another bold smile and bright eyes his way. This time, however, his stony reaction disappointed her, as did his reply.

'Mozart,' he said. 'I like Mozart.'

'A man of taste,' Byron affirmed gruffly.

'Mozart,' Jade pouted. '*God*!'

What a pompous jerk, she thought as she whirled away. I'll bet he just said that because he thought it would please Pops. I'll give him Mozart!

Shortly a heavy-metal number reverberated through the high-ceilinged room, turned up so loud it shook the chandelier overhead.

'Turn that infernal rubbish off!' Byron shouted.

'Sorry,' Jade apologised carelessly over her shoulder. 'Wrong CD. I don't have my glasses on.'

'You don't *wear* glasses,' her father bit out.

'Don't I? I'm sure I should. Big thick ones! Then I wouldn't be able to see all the cruelty in this miserable rotten world of ours.'

'*Jade*,' her father warned through gritted teeth.

Mozart floated through the room and Jade found her chair, opposite Kyle's. She went to throw him another saucy smile, but suddenly it changed to a very bleak one. Her own cynical words of a moment ago had brought memories of the newsflashes she'd seen all week on television about the starving children in Africa, their emaciated bodies tearing at her heartstrings.

What kind of world was it that allowed such misery, such suffering? She'd sent the Save The Children Fund some money but had still been left feeling depressed. Why was it always innocent children who suffered the most? Her eyes suddenly misted over and she looked down very quickly, blinking rapidly.

She was just getting herself under control when their guest went into a fit of coughing, forcing her to look up before she was fully composed. Her reaction was a most unsympathetic irritation.

What on earth was wrong with him? It didn't seem likely that Mr Cool was having an attack of asthma, or was allergic to the flowers on the table.

'Are you all right?' the others asked.

He flicked open his serviette and pressed it briefly against watering eyes. It annoyed Jade that, even watering, his eyes were gorgeous. The man was a menace, projecting sex appeal in waves even when he was coughing and spluttering like a smoker on his last inhale.

'I'm fine,' he choked out. 'Something went down the wrong way.'

What? she thought crossly. He hadn't started eating yet.

The soup arrived at that moment—another of Melanie's famous home-made varieties. The first of Byron's wines was poured and soon everyone was as mellow as Melanie's superb cooking and the best of Australia's vineyards could make the stressed inhabitants of the twentieth century. Jade, of course, drank far too much, too quickly. Consequently, she became more and more naughty as the night wore on. Not so much in what she said, but in the way she looked at the man seated opposite her.

Drunks often said the bartender got better looking as the night wore on. Kyle Armstrong definitely became more attractive as the night wore on, yet at the same time more unattainable. He was like a mirage, or the spectre in a dream that kept scooting away, out of her grasp. More and more he avoided her eyes and deflected her attempts to chat him up.

'When do you start work for Whitmore Opals?' she persisted over dessert, a mouth-watering chocolate pudding with lashings of cream.

'Monday,' came his cool reply.

'*This* Monday?'

'Mmm.'

'I've always wanted to work for Whitmore's in marketing,' she muttered into her wine. Frustration and alcohol were propelling Jade to a point somewhere between depression and aggression.

'Not that again, Jade,' her father sighed. 'If I've told you once, I've told you a thousand times. When you've attained your degree, I'll think about it.'

Jade's glassy blue eyes shot up. '*Think* about it! What do you mean, *think* about it? You told me if I got my degree you'd definitely give me a job. Are you trying to go back on our deal?'

'You know my feelings on women in business, Jade,' he said. 'Besides, I've employed Kyle now and I can't see him wanting some green assistant who'd probably hinder more than help.'

She pushed the rest of her pudding away, really upset now. 'But you *promised*!' she burst out.

'Jade, for God's sake, not now!'

'If I may speak, Byron?' Mr Cool inserted smoothly.

'Of course, Kyle. I'm just sorry you have to be exposed to our family squabbles like this.'

'I've worked for family companies all my life. I'm used to the occasional squabble. Might I say, however, that if things at Whitmore Opals are faring as badly as you've told me then I will need as many new marketing ideas as I can muster. A young, innovative brain like Jade's here would be an invaluable asset, even on a part-time basis. Not only that, we can be assured she would have Whitmore's best interests at heart. Since we have a formidable foe in Celeste Campbell, then there is always the chance of an employee being bribed or corrupted. We wouldn't have to worry about loyalty with your daughter, Byron. Frankly, I was thinking of hiring someone young to assist me and Jade would be the perfect person.'

He turned that implacable dark gaze on to her startled blue eyes and, once again, she felt the power of his mind. Here was a man who could not be forced into doing anything he didn't want to do, but likewise, who would be unstoppable once he'd made up his mind to achieve some end. It underlined the futility of her throwing herself at him when it was patently clear he wasn't interested in her in that way. Suddenly, she felt ashamed of herself for continuing to try after he'd made his feelings quite clear. It was beneath her. It was belittling. And cheap.

Jade sucked in a startled breath. *Cheap*? My God, she was beginning to sound like her own father!

'You must have some days off from lectures, Jade,' Kyle was saying. 'At least a morning or afternoon here and there. If not, there's always the weekends.'

A surge of excitement rushed through her. What Kyle was offering was better than the satisfying of her passing fancy for him. It was the career she'd always wanted, the life she'd always secretly coveted. Who knew? In a few years, she might give Celeste Campbell a run for her money.

'I...I have Wednesdays off,' she said eagerly. 'And Friday afternoons.'

'Good. Then I will expect to see you at head office next Wednesday morning. Nine, on the dot.'

Jade blinked several times, then turned to her father, who rolled his eyes. 'Pops?'

His sigh was resigned. 'I promised Kyle a free hand. If he wants to risk the likes of you, then so be it. I can only say I admire his fortitude.'

'Fortitude, Byron?' An odd smile crossed the new marketing manager's face. 'Fortitude has nothing to do with my hiring your daughter. Destiny is more like it.'

'Destiny?' Ava piped up, frowning. 'Whose destiny, Mr Armstrong?'

'Why, Jade's, of course,' he replied silkily. 'She stands to inherit Whitmore's at some future date, does she not, Byron? Or did I get my wires crossed this afternoon?'

Both women's eyes turned to Byron, Jade's the most round. So she *was* going to inherit Whitmore's. Nathan hadn't wangled the company for himself yet.

'No, you didn't get your wires crossed. Jade inherits the family business, though if we can't do something to turn the tables on our competition in the next year or so it won't be worth much.'

'Then it's about time she learnt the business,' Mr Cool pronounced. 'Time you took your future into your own hands, wouldn't you say, Jade?'

'Yes.' She beamed agreement and excitement at him. 'Oh, yes!'

Byron laughed. 'Don't give her too many ideas, Kyle. She's likely to run with them.'

'That's exactly what I want her to do.'

'What if she runs right off a cliff, like one of those lemmings?'

'Then I'll be there to catch her, Byron. I wouldn't let anything bad ever happen to your daughter. You can be assured of that.'

Jade bristled at the dry flavour she heard in that last statement. She didn't doubt he meant every word. The boss's daughter would always be cosseted and protected and pandered to. Pity he wasn't the type who was prepared to go even further to curry favour, she thought with a resurgence of pique. But he was too prim and proper for that. Too damned conservative and holier-than-thou. Trust her father to employ a prude!

'I don't want any special treatment,' she said sharply. 'I'm not doing this just to amuse myself, you know. I'm dead serious about learning everything you can teach me.'

'And I'm dead serious about teaching you everything I know,' Kyle returned, an odd note in his voice. Irony, perhaps?

Jade stared at him. A small warning prickle at the back of her neck made her sit up straight. She rolled her shoulders in an effort to dispel a sudden tension between her shoulder-blades. Had she missed something here? Why did she suddenly suspect there had been more to this exchange than appeared on the surface?

Melanie's drifting in to take the dessert plates away and ask who wanted tea or coffee obliterated the moment and Jade dismissed it as an aberration of her fuzzy state of mind. By the time everyone was on their second round of coffee she'd sobered right up, her revitalised brain already harnessing all sorts of marketing ideas for Whitmore Opals.

I'll have to start writing them down, she told herself, her earlier wild burst of excitement having been replaced by the calmer realisation that she must not waste this wonderful chance. And while a slight nervousness crept in at the prospect of working with and for Mr Cool, she resolved to do her very best.

Which meant she would have to ignore this unfortunate physical effect he had on her. OK, so he was gorgeous-looking and irritatingly sexy and even intriguing, in a way. But trying to seduce one's boss was not the way to impress him with her business acumen. This was her one chance to show her father she could be an invaluable asset to Whitmore Opals and she wasn't about to muff it by letting a little thing like sexual desire get in the way.

So what if she wanted the man to make love to her? So what if she wanted to make love to *him*? So what if the thought of either possibility was sending goosebumps all over her skin? So damned what!

Jade clenched her teeth down hard in her jaw, thankful that the jacket she had on was lined. Thinking such thoughts was doing scandalous things to her breasts. Dammit, but this wasn't going to be easy, not easy at all. The man had cast a spell on her. He was a Svengali, with dark powers to enslave and compel. Thank the lord he didn't realise it!

Good God, why was he getting to his feet? Surely he wasn't *going*! What had he just said to her? *Had* he said anything to her? Had she answered? She'd been off in

another world, her body working on automatic pilot
whilst her mind had been dancing with the devil.

He was looking at her as though he were expecting
her to say something. Well, *say something*, you little
nincompoop.

'I'll see you Wednesday, then?' she tried.

Everyone stared at her.

'What's the matter with you, girl?' Byron snapped.
'You just agreed to walk Kyle to the door and open the
gates for him.'

Her laughter was self-mocking as she stood up and
moved across to the doorway. Kyle was right on her
hammer.

'Call me from the office on Monday morning, Kyle,'
Byron called after him.

'Certainly.'

Jade tried very hard to be the epitome of social grace
as she walked Kyle towards the front door. It was as
though this was her first test in controlling herself and
acting like a mature young lady. She didn't walk too
fast, she said all the right things—wonderfully polite in-
anities she would not recall later. She even remembered
to press the remote control on the wall that opened the
gates before she escorted their visitor through the front
door and out on to the well-lit front patio. Why, there
wasn't anything she couldn't do, Jade decided.

Her faith in herself was a little premature.

The moment Kyle turned to her and took her hand in
his—no doubt only as a gesture of goodbye—she lost
the plot entirely. Did he really squeeze her fingers? Did
those dark eyes darken with desire for her? Surely it
wasn't her imagination that his stillness was suddenly
projecting a sexual tension that was so palpable she could
feel it in every pore of her body.

'Kyle,' she whispered in automatic response, his name
a husky plea of raw arousal.

She could have sworn his fingers tightened even further
for a second, that his mouth dipped slightly toward hers.
But then he was saying goodnight in cold clipped tones

and was walking away, away from her parted panting lips, away from her madly pounding heart.

Jade watched, dry-mouthed and stunned, as he drove off in a silver-grey sedan, a super-cool car for its super-cool driver. He hadn't given her a backward glance, or a wave, or even a smile. He'd given her nothing but his hard cold back.

I hate him, she decided. And flounced inside.

CHAPTER FIVE

NATHAN directed his navy blue Mercedes through the gates of Belleview shortly after seven-thirty on Sunday evening. Kirsty had slept most of the day, exhausted by her movie marathon the night before. Gemma and Nathan hadn't been much brighter, equally exhausted with their own marathon. The trip home had been slow, the freeway choked with cars returning to Sydney from a weekend up on the coast.

Gemma locked eyes with Nathan in the rear-view mirror as he directed the car round to the garages.

Keep your head, his steely glance seemed to say.

She looked away, all her insides tightening into tangled knots. She hated having to pretend to people she liked, hated to think that one day soon Kirsty and Melanie and Ava—and even Byron—would look at her with shock and disappointment in their eyes. She shuddered to think what Lenore might say as well, still not sure how Nathan's ex-wife felt about her ex-husband. Nathan might not love *her*, but did she still love *him*?

'Home at last,' Kirsty yawned. 'I'm really bushed. Just as well I don't do that every weekend.'

'I think it might be wise if you didn't tell your mother about last night, Kirsty,' her father warned.

Kirsty grinned. 'What she doesn't know won't hurt her, eh, Dad?'

Gemma groaned silently. Out of the mouths of babes...

'Everyone carry their own bags,' Nathan directed crisply as they all climbed out of the car.

'I'm going straight to bed,' Kirsty said with another yawn.

'I've got a bit of Japanese study to do before tomorrow,' Gemma admitted.

Kirsty frowned at her. 'I thought that was what you were doing all day today.'

Gemma could feel the heat gathering in her cheeks, which was crazy since she and Nathan hadn't done a thing today. They hadn't dared, with Kirsty in the house. There again, if she admitted to resting most of the day that might lead Kirsty asking what she'd been doing the previous night to make her so tired. 'I...I couldn't seem to concentrate,' she hedged. 'I had a headache.'

'You might have got a touch of the sun yesterday,' Kirsty said, lifting out her bag which was on top of the pile in the boot. 'That can give you a headache sometimes. You should drink a lot of water and take a couple of aspirin before going to bed. Well, I'm off. Thanks heaps, Dad, for letting me do you know what. You're a cool dude. See you in the morning, Gemma.'

Kirsty kissed her father on the cheek then was gone, using the internal door that connected the garages with the laundry and kitchen wing of the house. Gemma was still standing there beside the car when Nathan banged down the boot, then slid her a drily amused look.

'A headache, eh?' he drawled. 'I hope that isn't going to become a standard excuse of the future Mrs Whitmore.'

Before she could fashion a reply, he leant over, cupped her chin and kissed her—not at all lightly—on the mouth. He'd just lifted his head when the sound of hurried footsteps had them both whirling to stare at the still open doorway that Kirsty had gone through.

Jade didn't have to be Sherlock Holmes to guess what she'd just missed seeing. If their guilty movements hadn't given them away, then she only had to look at the flush on the girl's face and the frustration in Nathan's eyes to know there'd been some surreptitious canoodling going on.

Not that she cared.

Jade sucked in a sharp breath. My God, she didn't care. She actually didn't. How marvellous!

Her smile carried a startled delight. 'So there you are, Nathan. I've been sweating on your getting back. I have a favour to ask of you.'

Nathan's scowl was predictable, but the girl's fiercely jealous glare took Jade by surprise. So things had gone that far already, had they? Sympathy for the poor thing's predicament soon replaced any shock. Jade had been in the same position not that long ago, hopelessly besotted with the man and hating any woman who so much as looked at him, let alone took up his time.

'Hello there,' Jade said sweetly. 'You're Gemma, aren't you? Do you remember me? I'm Jade, Nathan's sister.' Maybe if she dropped the adopted part, the girl would stop looking so threatened.

'Of course she remembers you,' Nathan ground out. 'You're not easily forgotten, Jade. What do you want? You aren't going to move back here to live, are you?'

'No, darls,' she said automatically before she could snatch back her usual meaningless endearment. The girlfriend didn't realise how meaningless, of course, and was looking none too happy. Beautiful, though. God, yes, she was a stunner all right. Jade just managed not to feel envious, concentrating instead on the improvement her own life would make next Wednesday. Hating Kyle Armstrong didn't change the fact that he'd hired her as his marketing assistant and she just couldn't wait to start!

But her more immediate problem was getting Roberto out of her unit. Hopefully, by now, his so-called friends—including her attacker—had gone back to their own caves. But she couldn't be sure of that, and returning to her unit on her own was just too scary, even for her.

'Look, I know you're probably tired and I hate to ask, but I need you to go with me back to my unit. I have to evict a friend who's turned out to be a problem and I'm afraid he might need some persuasion.'

'Is it Roberto? Or someone new?' Nathan added in a nasty tone.

'Roberto.' God, but she was going to enjoy enlightening him about Roberto's sexuality. She was getting sick and tired of Nathan pointing a moral finger at her when he was obviously racing off this sweet young thing under everyone's noses. How dared he judge her, the cradle-snatching lecher?

Nathan sighed. 'I supposed we might as well get this over and done with and go now.'

'Really? Gosh, thanks.' She beamed. For all his faults, Nathan usually came through if one asked nicely. 'I'll just get my car keys.'

She scuttled away, thinking magnanimously that this would give the lovebirds a chance to say a proper—or improper—goodnight. When she got back, Gemma had disappeared and Nathan was leaning against the driver's door of his car, an impatient glint in his eye.

'I hope you don't expect me to rough up this boyfriend of yours, Jade. I gave up that sort of thing when I was seventeen.'

'I doubt anything of that kind will be necessary with Roberto, Nathan. He's basically a gentle soul. Unfortunately, one of his friends wasn't.'

Nathan frowned and stood up straight. 'Meaning?'

For some reason Jade couldn't quite meet his eye. A trembling started deep within and, try as she might to stop the memory of the assault from unnerving her, she found that all of a sudden she was very jittery. 'I...I...'

'What? Spit it out, for God's sake.'

His impatience infuriated her. 'I was almost raped!' she blurted out, shaking now, though whether from anger or fear, Jade wasn't sure. 'Luckily, I got away from the filthy creep and I...I came here.'

'On Friday night?'

'That's right.'

'At least that explains the car in the fishpond,' he muttered, shaking his head at her as though it were *her* fault she'd been attacked. 'I knew this would happen one day. I hope you've learnt your lesson, and stop inviting every Tom, Dick and Harry to move in with you at the drop of a hat.'

'I don't do that! I've *never* done that. I'll have you know that Roberto is not my boyfriend, *or* my lover. He was just a friend in need of a room for a while. He's also gay. He had a few friends over on Friday night for a party. Not that I attended. I went to bed. Later in the night, I got up for a drink of water. I...I thought everyone had gone home. Apparently not, however.'

Nathan stared at her for a few moments before speaking. 'Was this man who attacked you also gay?'

'I'm not sure, but he certainly led me to believe he hated women. You should have heard the things he said he was going to do to me while he was trying to drag me from the kitchen to the bedroom.' She shuddered violently.

'But you got away before he really hurt you?' Nathan asked, anxiety in his voice.

'My breasts were bruised.' She undid a couple of buttons of her shirt and showed him some of the black and blue marks.

'Good God.' His eyes showed real shock and Jade found it hard not to dissolve into tears.

'I presume you haven't told Byron any of this?' he asked more gently.

'Of course not. Do you think I'm stupid?'

A wry smile crossed his handsome face. 'I think you're crazy. But I also think you're very lucky, *and* very brave.'

'Not really, I've spent the whole weekend trying to pretend it never happened. If I didn't have to go back to that flat, I wouldn't. I doubt I'll ever be able to go into the kitchen again without reliving it all.'

'Then don't go back.'

Jade gaped at him.

'You're only renting, aren't you?'

'Yes.'

'And the unit came furnished?'

'Yes.'

'So you only have to remove your clothes and give back the keys to have done with the place.'

'Not really. My lease won't be up for another few months.'

'That's just a matter of money, Jade. I'll fix that up.'

'But I can't allow you to do that! It would run into a couple of thousand dollars. Surely you've got enough expense what with paying Lenore alimony and... and—'

'Jade,' he interrupted. 'I think it's time you knew I'm no longer the deprived stray from the streets your father brought home. I do not have to make ends meet on the salary your father pays me, or via the iffy financial rewards that my plays occasionally bring in. My maternal grandparents, despite refusing to have anything personal to do with me after they disinherited my mother, still saw fit to make me their heir. A few years back I inherited a considerable estate, so I think I can well afford to extricate my favourite adopted sister from a sticky situation, don't you?'

'F... favourite adopted sister?' Jade repeated, a lump in her throat.

Nathan's smile was rather sad. 'Favourite and only adopted sister. I wish you'd go back to filling that role, Jade. I rather liked being your big brother. Anything else felt all wrong, even if you were an incredible temptation there for a while. You'd be an incredible temptation to any man.'

Jade hid her pleasure behind a dry laugh. 'I know one particular man who wouldn't agree with you.'

Now Nathan laughed, and it was just as dry. 'Not another man, Jade. Good God, doesn't anything turn you off the opposite sex? Still, I'm relieved I've been taken off the list, but I pity the poor sod—whoever he is. No, don't tell me, just give me the keys to your flat and I'll go sort Roberto out and come back with your clothes.'

'You... you'd really do that for me?'

'I'm your big brother, aren't I?'

Her heart contracted. 'Forever and ever.'

Gemma was sitting on the side of her bed, feeling woebegone and abandoned when there was a knock on her door. Going to answer it, she found Jade standing there, looking as raunchily sexy as ever, skin-tight jeans and a man's white shirt doing little to disguise that spectacular body of hers.

'I thought I'd better warn you,' Jade said. 'Nathan might be a good while. He's gone to get my clothes from my unit at Avalon. I'm going to be staying at Belleview here for a while.'

Gemma felt totally confused. 'But I thought you said that . . . that . . .

'That I wouldn't be moving back home,' the girl finished with a sigh. 'Yes, I know, but I had this problem with a man last Friday night which was rather serious and Nathan feels it would be safer if I stayed here for a while. I dare say I'll find another place in the near future, but I have to admit it feels good to be home in the meantime.'

Gemma's heart sank. What was it about the women in Nathan's life that he castigated them to her in private, but then his actions didn't match his words? Lenore got under his skin, but he'd *kissed* her. He was highly critical of Jade and said he would not have her under the same roof as his daughter but here he was, helping to bring that about. In fact, it sounded as if it was *his* idea.

She was startled when Jade suddenly put a gentle hand on hers. 'Please don't think I'm a rival for Nathan's affections,' the girl said softly. 'I admit I had a crush on him once, but I'm over that now and quite frankly I would like nothing more than for him to fall in love with a really nice girl like you.'

Gemma was taken aback by the girl's compliment, and her intuitive comment about her and Nathan. 'How . . . how would you know if I'm a nice girl or not?' she asked tentatively.

Jade smiled. 'I've been listening to Ava and Melanie singing your praises all weekend. To be honest, I was quite prepared to hate you on sight, but I don't seem to be able to rustle up the necessary emotion. Maybe I'm all out of hate or maybe this weekend has made me grow up a little. In the space of two days, I've fought off a rapist, survived being rejected by a man I *did* fancy and then was spectacularly hired for a job I've always coveted. I'm feeling too good to hate.'

She grinned at Gemma, who shook her head. 'You're crazy.'

Jade laughed. 'Crazy is as crazy does, darls. Let's go down to the kitchen and have some hot chocolate, and then you can tell me your life story.' Linking elbows with Gemma, she started railroading her from the room. Surrender seemed the safest course of action.

'I think yours might be more interesting than mine,' Gemma said.

'Nah. Mine's been miserable, but it's looking up. Yes. It's very definitely looking up.'

'You really fought off a rapist?'

'Yup. Kicked the creep in the balls.'

'Good lord! Weren't you afraid?'

'Scared to death. But madder than a meat-axe at the same time.'

'And who was this man who rejected you?' Gemma asked, finding it hard to see any man daring to reject this wildly attractive creature.

'Some stuffed shirt named Kyle Armstrong. He's the new marketing manager at Whitmore Opals and he came here to dinner last night. Talk about scrumptious-looking! But batting my baby blues at him just didn't work. Still, he knew what side his bread was buttered on, my being the daughter of the boss and all. So he's hired me to be his part-time assistant till I finish my business degree this year which is what I've always wanted.'

'You're doing a business degree?'

'Well, you don't have to sound so surprised, darls. I'm a smart cookie underneath the bleached hair and big boobs.'

Gemma stared at her hair.

'Yes, the hair's fake but the boobs aren't. They're all mine.'

'I...I...'

'Close your mouth, darls, or you'll start catching flies. Now tell me, how did a nice girl like you get to be living in a den of iniquity like Belleview? No lies now, I want the truth, the whole truth and nothing but the truth!'

By the time Nathan returned over an hour later, Gemma had just got to the part where Nathan had told her the disappointing news about her mother, though she had, naturally, omitted her personal involvement with him. Nathan would be furious with her if she let the cat out of the bag, especially to Jade. That girl didn't know how to shut up!

'I thought you'd be in bed by now, Gemma,' Nathan said on entering the kitchen via the door that led to the laundry and the garages.

'She was waiting for you, darls,' Jade said naughtily before adding, 'To come back, that is. We've had the loveliest long chat about Gemma's colourful life up till now. Fancy all that business about her father's having that opal belonging to Pops. You know . . . the one called the Heart of Fire.'

'I know the one.'

'But what a coincidence! And what a shame her birth certificate is packed full of lies. Poor Gemma probably won't ever find her mother's family now, will she? Or even know her mother's real name? Are you sure you can't do something about that? Hire a private investigator or something? They have access to all sorts of information us ordinary people can't tap into.'

'I intend doing that, Jade. Don't pre-empt me. Don't you want to know what happened at your unit with Roberto?'

'Not if you did anything violent?'

'Didn't have to. Once I pointed out what might happen to him and his friends if he stayed one minute longer, he left like a lamb.'

'Poor Roberto . . .'

'Keep your sympathy for someone who deserves it, Jade. Now how about you two girls coming along to the garage and help me empty my car of madam's gear?'

'You make it sound as if I've got tons!' Jade complained. 'I don't have that many clothes. I live in jeans and shorts.'

'I brought all the linen as well. I've got a bootful of towels and sheets and quilts and God knows what. Most of them need washing so we'll just pile them into the laundry and you can help Melanie sort them out tomorrow.'

'I have lectures first thing in the morning,' Jade said.

'I could help after I get home from my Japanese lessons,' Gemma offered.

'Would you?' Jade smiled her appreciation. 'Oh, you are a dear. She's a dear, isn't she, Nathan?'

'Yes, she is, so don't take advantage of her.'

'Talk about the pot calling the kettle black,' Jade muttered under her breath after Nathan had whirled and stalked back down the corridor towards the garages.

Gemma pretended she hadn't heard, but she had, and the reasoning behind the remark worried her.

Jade knew about them. Not only knew but had made her judgement. Nathan had once again been cast in the role of callous seducer. Wasn't there anyone around Belleview who had faith in his ability to love a woman? Anyone besides herself?

Gemma frowned, mulling over the thought that all these other people had known Nathan a lot longer than she had. Was she being naïve believing he meant to marry her? Was he stringing her along merely to have sex with her? Was that why he wanted to keep their engagement a secret?

Her head told her she had reason to worry, but her heart was strong in Nathan's defence. He loved her and meant to marry her. She felt sure of it.

Still...it wouldn't do any harm not to be too easy when it came to letting Nathan make love to her, especially here at Belleview. He said they would be married within a month, five weeks at the most. A man genuinely in love could wait that long, couldn't he?

Gemma hoped so. She herself would find such a sacrifice quite hard. Nathan making love to her was the most wonderful experience in the world. But they had all their lives ahead of them if his intentions were honourable and true, and Gemma would not want to marry any other kind of man. She wasn't so besotted that every ounce of her common sense had flown out the window.

Her mind made up, she picked up her empty mug and glanced over at Jade, who seemed lost in her own thoughts. 'You finished with your mug, Jade?' she asked.

'What? Oh, yes . . . yes, I have. But you don't have to wash it up for me. I'll do it.'

'It's no trouble.' Gemma swept the other mug up off the counter and made for the kitchen sink.

'Gemma . . .' the other girl began tentatively.

'Yes?'

'Oh . . . nothing. I . . . I'd better get to bed or I'll be wrecked tomorrow. Goodnight. And thanks again. You're a doll.'

Gemma watched Jade walk away, still amazed at how much she liked her. If Jade had once been in love with Nathan she certainly wasn't now, which was a relief. The girl was a walking sex symbol.

Maybe she was one of those girls who fell in and out of love a lot. Gemma had known a few like that at school. A good-looking boy only had to smile at them and they were crazy about them, their previous boyfriend forgotten. Then the following week there would be someone else.

Gemma had never been like that. There again, she'd found most boys at school boring and immature and highly unattractive. She'd never even had one serious boyfriend.

Gemma had always suspected she found the opposite sex unappealing because of that awful night as a young girl when that drunken miner had sexually assaulted her, his attack only falling short of rape because he'd been too drunk to do it.

But now, looking back, she could see not having a boyfriend had more to do with her real age than wariness. She'd been two years older than her classmates. Emotionally, she'd been even older.

Nathan's news that her birth certificate was a legitimate one had not changed her mind about her true age.

She wasn't eighteen. She was nearly twenty, or already twenty by now. That photo of her mother and father proved it, as it proved her father a liar. The more she thought about her father, the more she was convinced he was not only a liar but a thief. He'd stolen that black opal. That was why he hadn't sold it, why he'd hidden it away.

How he'd managed to execute the original theft here at Belleview all those years ago she couldn't fathom. Maybe he'd had an accomplice. Whatever, she was sure he'd been criminally involved, which was why he'd been so secretive about everything, why he'd lied about things.

Thinking of her father and the opal reminded Gemma that she must give that photo of her parents to Nathan. But not tonight. Going to his room at night was courting disaster. No, she would give it to him at breakfast. And she wouldn't be going to Avoca with him any more either. Not till after they were married. Gemma had a point to prove to herself and she was going to prove it, come hell or high water!

Having washed up the two mugs, she made her way upstairs, thinking to herself that Ma would be very proud of her.

CHAPTER SIX

BY THE following Wednesday morning Jade was in a state of nervous agitation which wasn't entirely due to her starting work that day. Living at home was proving to be a trial of the first order.

She found it hard to resume the role of daughter of the house, especially with her father in such a frustrated mood. She'd become used to running her own race, without having to put up with any criticism, especially about what she wore or the hours she kept. Even Ava's well-meaning pieces of advice began to grate after a while.

Frankly, Jade felt extra irritated with her aunt, who had refused her offer of Irene's jewellery, saying she wouldn't feel right about it. Clearly, there was no hope for Auntie Ava. She seemed determined to grow old playing the part of the unattractive, eccentric spinster of the family, stuffing her face with cream buns while dreaming of imaginary beaux that got away.

On top of all those irritations, Jade felt uneasy with what was going on between Nathan and Gemma.

They were certainly putting on a good act with their platonic conversations and avoidance of any telling eye contact, but Jade's bedroom was opposite Nathan's and she'd heard the soft sound of his door opening and shutting very late the previous night.

Because she'd been too excited about starting work to sleep, she'd still been awake when, even later, she'd heard more sounds. Slipping from her bed, she'd snuck over and opened her door an inch or two just in time to see a scantily clad Gemma high-tailing it back into her room. And she hadn't been coming from the direction of downstairs!

Jade had found it even harder to go to sleep after that, because like everyone else around Belleview she'd found herself growing very fond of Gemma with her country-sweet and very caring ways. Despite her own reconciliation with Nathan—and a new appreciation of her adopted brother's strength of character—Jade still felt the girl deserved better in life than to get involved with a man as emotionally screwed up as Nathan was, not to mention as sexually dangerous.

Did he himself appreciate how infatuated a young girl like Gemma could get in double-quick time? She was sure to think she was madly in love, especially with her limited experience with men. She probably thought Nathan was in love with *her*. God forbid, he might have told her he was, for who knew what a man might say when in the throes of a new passion?

Jade didn't like to judge Nathan too harshly—he hadn't turned out to be as heartless as she'd once imagined—but he did still have his limitations when it came to relationships with women. Lenore had confided to Jade shortly after their divorce that all Nathan wanted from a wife was an elegant partner on his arm and a willing body in bed. No true intimacy or companionship. He'd even told her once that if she hadn't fallen pregnant with Kirsty he would never have married her at all, nor any other woman for that matter.

Lenore had confessed that she might have been able to put up with all this—Nathan was apparently so good in bed that the woman was almost prepared to put up with anything!—but it seemed that when he was consumed by a creative burst with a new play Lenore had found herself denied even the small consolation of a good sex life. Writing, it seemed, involved Nathan to the exclusion of everyone and everything else.

Jade suspected that there was an element behind Lenore and Nathan's divorce that still remained hidden, but the main thrust was pretty straightforward. Nathan had made a lousy husband.

Thank the lord Jade didn't have to worry about Nathan rushing Gemma off to some altar somewhere.

He'd always made his feelings on remarrying quite clear. Still, that didn't mean Gemma wouldn't ultimately get hurt, and this upset Jade. The poor darling had had a rough time of it so far in life and she deserved a break. Hell, there she'd been, thinking she'd inherited a fantastic opal from that rotten dead-beat father of hers and what had happened? It had turned out to be stolen from none other than Jade's own father. Pops might have given Gemma a nice reward for the opal's return, but what was a hundred thousand dollars compared to a million? One was a nice little nest egg, but the other would have set Gemma up for life.

Jade was mulling over all these thoughts as she headed downstairs for breakfast, resolving to drop a few subtle hints to Nathan when she got the chance. Maybe he didn't realise how naïve and impressionable Gemma was.

Or maybe he did, came another far more disturbing, darker thought. God, if Nathan did anything to really hurt that girl she was going to tear strips off him! Come to think of it, she would accept his offer of a lift to work this morning. She'd been going to drive herself, liking her independence, but riding into town with Nathan would give her a great opportunity to find out how things stood.

'All ready for your first assault on the business world?' the man himself said when Jade walked into the morning-room. 'You certainly look the part in that outfit. I've never seen you looking so—er...' He broke off, frowning. 'What have I said to make you glare at me like that? I wasn't making fun of you, I swear. That black suit looks fantastic on you.'

Jade wiped the scowl off her face and rewarded him with an insincere smile. Hypocrisy never did come easy to her. If she was angry with someone it showed on her face, not the best thing if she was going to become a businesswoman. No doubt Celeste Campbell had the best poker face in the whole of Australia.

'Sorry,' she said. 'I'm a bit out of sorts this morning. Guess it's nerves. Where's Gemma? Sleeping in, is she?'

Oh, dear, did that sound as pointedly sarcastic as she thought it did?

'How would *I* know?' His shrug was superbly nonchalant and Jade's level of worry increased.

Damn, but he was a clever devil. And too darned handsome for his own good. He and Kyle Armstrong made a good pair.

Kyle Armstrong...

Jade's mind was suddenly filled with that brooding gypsy face and those glittering black eyes. She would be seeing him today, would be spending most of the day with him. Hell.

Reminding herself of Whitmore's new marketing manager blocked out all thought of Gemma and Nathan for the rest of breakfast. In fact, Jade was so distracted she almost forgot to tell Nathan she'd decided to accompany him into the city. Only Gemma and Kirsty coming downstairs reminded her to speak up.

Gemma looked unhappy with the news. Surely she's still not worried I'm interested in Nathan, Jade frowned to herself.

Whatever, the girl's jealous reaction underlined the very things Jade had been worrying about earlier. Gemma might think herself mature at nearly twenty, but she was light-years behind a city born and bred girl of the same age. And a *zillion* light-years behind Nathan!

'Gee, Jade, you look smashing,' Kirsty said as she pulled out a chair and sat down.

'Yes, Jade,' Gemma agreed, though not quite as enthusiastically. 'You certainly do.'

Jade hoped her smile was as soothing as her words. 'How nice of you both to say so. I was thinking I was a bit overdressed. Lenore directed me to a boutique that specialises in the smart working-girl look and I splashed out on three suits. One black, one white and one red, all of which I can mix and match.'

'Really? Where is this boutique?' Gemma asked, her interest quite genuine. 'I'm going to need some clothes for work.'

'Chatswood. I could take you there tomorrow night if you like.'

The girl frowned. 'Tomorrow *night*?'

'It's late-night shopping. I suppose you didn't have that up at Lightning Ridge.'

'No, we didn't.'

'I'll get Lenore to come with us,' Jade suggested. 'She knows heaps about fashion and what suits a person.' It was slowly coming to Jade that it was her super-smart appearance that had troubled Gemma, who admittedly still looked very young in her clothes, even the ones Ava had given her. Ava's taste had always leant towards the cute and pretty rather than the elegant or sophisticated.

'Gemma looks fine as she is,' Nathan said in a voice and with a look that totally betrayed his feelings for his daughter's minder. Not only possessive, but fiercely protective of the person she was right at this moment. He didn't want her tampered with in any way, or changed, or made over.

Jade resolved to do all three as quickly as possible, for only by widening the girl's horizons and opening her eyes a little could she be saved from Nathan's selfish male desires. Even if he imagined he loved the girl, it was not a healthy type of love if it didn't allow Gemma to grow, if it tried to imprison her in a narrow world where all that was to exist for her was his wishes. Jade hated the way men liked to dominate and control the women they supposedly loved. Real love didn't have reins.

'That's for Gemma to say, surely, Nathan,' Jade retorted, seeing the girl's instant frown. 'She's not a child. Even if she was, you're neither her father nor her big brother, so your opinion doesn't count.' She threw Gemma a dazzling smile. 'I'll get in touch with Lenore today, Gemma, and we'll make a date to buy you some working clothes tomorrow evening. When do you start being a super salesgirl, anyway?'

'In about a month.'

'The time will fly by.'

'I hope so.' The wistful tone in the girl's voice didn't escape Jade and she vowed to take the girl out and about a lot more. Gemma needed a girlfriend, that was clear, someone she could perhaps confide in. Jade had loads of advice for any unfortunate female infatuated with Nathan. After all, she had first-hand experience of the disease. With a bit of luck, Lenore might drop the odd antidotal remark about her ex as well.

By the time Nathan angled his car out of the driveway and into the traffic heading for the city—Jade firmly belted in the passenger seat—she was feeling quite angry with him. Though determined to tackle him on the subject of Gemma, she knew better than to simply blurt out a tactless accusation. Nathan would simply close up shop and tell her to mind her own damned business. She decided a comment about the weather was always a good place to start.

'Nice day,' she said.

'It's rather chilly in this car,' Nathan returned drily. 'Is it something I've done, or shall we blame first-day nerves?'

'Chilly? I don't know what you mean?'

Nathan laughed. 'Come now, Jade, I've known you far too long not to pick up your airwaves. You're spoiling for a fight but just aren't sure where to start.'

Jade's mouth thinned. If there was one thing she detested more than male chauvinists, it was when the devils were right! 'I admit I have a delicate problem which requires some subtlety of approach,' she said archly.

'Which lets you out, sweetheart. Subtlety is not your strong hand.'

Jade bristled. 'In that case, I'll bypass subtlety in favour of blunt honesty.' She dragged in a deep, courage-filling breath. 'I know you're sleeping with Gemma on the sly, Nathan, which is not only reprehensible considering Gemma's obvious inexperience with men, but in appalling bad taste with your fourteen-year-old daughter just down the hallway.'

The stillness and the silence in the car was mind-numbing. After a minute had passed Jade could not stand the strain another second.

'Say something, for heaven's sake!' she burst out.

His sidewards glance would have killed a brown snake at a hundred yards. 'I am still recovering from your gall,' he said in a voice dipped in liquid nitrogen.

'*My* gall!' Jade squeaked. 'At least I climbed out of the window for *my* assignations. I didn't have any of my boyfriends sleaze their way into my room in the dead of night.'

Nathan's inward breath sounded like a bellows with emphysema. It came to Jade she just might have over-stepped the mark.

'My God,' he snarled. 'If I hadn't heard it with my own ears I would not have believed it. Jade Whitmore, lecturing *me* on matters of morals. I'll have you know, Madam Lash, that I have spent the majority of my adult life stopping the women of the Whitmore family from sleazing their way into *my* bedroom in the dead of night. They've all made the offer at one time or another. But I did the right thing, every damned time. Even with you, who came along when I was sexually vulnerable. You, who draped herself all over me in a semi-naked state. *You*, who used every one of your considerable womanly wiles to seduce me! And yet here you are, with the effrontery to make a moral judgement on *me*!'

Guilt and confusion rattled Jade for a moment, but then she recognised Nathan's argument for what it was—a clever ruse to deflect her from the real issue at hand here. Which was the reality of his association with Gemma.

'I know I've been silly in the past, Nathan. But I'm not nearly as bad as either you or Pops think I am. I could count my lovers on the fingers of my left hand and still have a finger or two left over. But that's immaterial to what's going on between you and Gemma and you know it.'

Another silence descended on the car but this time it was Nathan who broke it, though his voice was no warmer than the last time.

'I'm only going to say this once, Jade. If there is something going on between Gemma and myself then it is nobody's business but Gemma's and mine. When you grew up, Jade, I accorded you the rights and privileges of being an adult, one of which is privacy. What you do in your own private life is your business, and what I do in mine is mine. Do I make myself clear?'

'Absolutely.'

'I sincerely hope you haven't been voicing these scurrilous suspicions of yours to others around Belleview.'

'Not as yet, but they may have already jumped to the same conclusions.'

'I doubt that very much.'

'Are you saying you haven't been sleeping with Gemma?'

'What makes you think I have?'

'I saw her leaving your room late last night.'

'We were just talking. She was worried about something.'

'I don't believe you.'

'It's the truth.' And he looked her straight in the eyes. Damn it, but she believed him.

'You mean you're not having an affair with her?' she quizzed, and watched his face some more.

'No,' he said solidly. 'I am not.'

'Well, I'll be blowed! I could have sworn you were.'

'If you say anything of the kind to Gemma she'll be horribly embarrassed. She's not as sophisticated as you, Jade. She'll want to curl up and die. She might even leave Belleview, and we don't want that, do we?'

'No, of course not. I won't say anything if you promise never to hurt that girl, Nathan. She's much too sweet for the likes of you.'

His laughter was dark. 'I promise never to hurt Gemma. There, will that do?'

'I suppose so. But watch it, I think she has a crush on you.'

'Do you, now?'

'Yes, I do.'

'One more thing while we're discussing Gemma, if you don't mind, Jade.'

'What?' she responded warily.

'This clothes-buying expedition you'll be going on with her. Don't let Lenore turn her into a clone of herself, will you? Gemma's charm lies in her being herself, in being unspoiled. Why change an original mould in favour of a mass-produced variety? Women like Lenore are a dime a dozen around Sydney.'

Jade stared over at him. 'I didn't realise how much you hated poor Lenore.'

'I don't hate her.'

'You could have fooled me.'

'Divorce is an ugly thing, Jade. It leaves scars.'

'Lenore carries a few of her own.'

Nathan laughed. 'You women always stick together.'

'So do you men.'

'You've become a feminist.'

'What do you mean...*become*? I haven't worn a bra in years.'

He slanted her a rueful smile. 'At least you can't tell under that jacket,' he said, his comment startlingly close to Byron's last time she'd dressed up.

'It wouldn't matter if you could,' came her dry reply. 'Braless breasts don't raise an eyebrow on the man I'll be working with today.'

'Is that so? Sounds as if your nose is out of joint a little. I didn't realise you'd met the inimitable Mr Armstrong.'

'I was home when he came visiting Pops last Saturday. He stayed for dinner.'

'But he didn't want you for afters?' Nathan mocked.

'Didn't even want a little nibble,' Jade admitted with a melodramatic sigh.

Nathan laughed. 'There's no accounting for bad taste, I suppose. Or maybe he's gay, like Roberto.'

Jade's head whipped round. 'Good grief, I never thought of that.' But when she did every feminine instinct within her screamed in protest. 'No,' she said confidently. 'He's not gay.'

'How can you tell?'

'I can tell, believe me. My female antennae wouldn't have worked so well if he had been. I dare say he has a girlfriend or lover stashed away somewhere. That's the problem. Our sexy new marketing manager is just not on the market.'

'You really found him sexy, Jade? I'm amazed. I thought he was rather cold and arrogant when I met him on Monday. But first impressions can be deceiving, I would also have said he'd been born with a silver spoon in his mouth and was no stranger to being sucked up to. Which shows how wrong one can be. His résumé revealed a more than ordinary background. A state school education, a business degree at the Hobart University, followed by seven years straight with the marketing section of an international food company, the last three as head of the division. A successful enough career but one which I didn't think matched his personality.'

'I couldn't agree more,' Jade drawled. 'The man's insufferably egotistical. But I have to admit he was clever with Pops. Called him sir and kowtowed beautifully without being at all obsequious.'

'Is that so? Mmm. Perhaps our Mr Armstrong bears close watching for a while.' Nathan was pensively silent for a minute then brightened, throwing Jade one of his double-sided smiles. 'But you'll have to do the watching, Jade. I'm finishing up at Whitmore's this week to write full time. Your father will be back at the helm next Monday.'

Jade liked nothing more than the thought of watching Kyle Armstrong closely. She was still as besotted, beguiled and bewitched by the man as she had been last Saturday. But the news that Nathan was permanently leaving Whitmore's came as a surprise, though not an entirely unwelcome one. She'd always been jealous of his relationship with her father and relished the idea of becoming closer to Byron herself, and proving she was every bit as clever and competent as her adopted brother.

'You're really leaving, Nathan?'

'Yup.'

'Will you stay living at Belleview?'

'Can't say that I will.'

Now this *was* good news. He could hardly seduce Gemma when they wouldn't even be under the same roof. Unless he planned to take both Kirsty and Gemma with him...

'I suppose you'll move up into the beach-house at Avoca,' she suggested sneakily, knowing that would mean Kirsty would have to go home to her mother to live. 'You've always been keen on that place and you seem to write well there.'

'Yes, that's definitely where I'll go.'

'What about Kirsty?'

Now he frowned. 'She'll have to go home to her mother, I suppose.'

'Well, that's where Kirsty is best off, surely. And Lenore loves her dearly, Nathan. She probably only wanted a break from her. Teenage girls can be a right pain in the neck, as you well know.' She grinned over at him in memory of her own hair-raising escapades.

Nathan grunted.

'Maybe Lenore will let Gemma live with them, since Kirsty's grown so fond of her minder. Actually, that might not be such a bad idea. I suppose you know Lenore's rehearsing a new play which starts in a couple of weeks. With her out most nights, she might like someone at home with Kirsty.'

'Lenore has a pensioner lady neighbour who sits with Kirsty whenever she has to be out at night. I doubt she will want a third person living in the house with them. Lenore values her privacy these days,' he finished with an acid tone that astonished and irritated Jade. Surely it was Nathan who had always valued privacy.

'Which rather leaves Gemma like a shag on a rock, doesn't it?' she retorted. 'You know the poor little thing doesn't have any friends or relatives in Sydney. Which reminds me, have you found out anything more about her mother or her folks?'

'Gemma gave me a photo she had and I've asked Zachary to hire an investigator he knows to make enquiries. As for Gemma herself, there's no reason why she can't stay on at Belleview indefinitely. Melanie and Ava like having her around.'

'Are you sure it's not you who likes having her around, Nathan?'

His smile sent icicles up and down Jade's spine. 'You don't give up easily, do you?'

'I'm not one to underestimate a man's sexual needs, Nathan,' came her cool reply, her mind flying to a mental image of her father and Mrs Parkes embracing and kissing. 'I haven't noticed you taking out any ladies lately. Yet you're not writing at the moment.'

His grey eyes hardened as they slid her way. 'My, you're an observant little thing, aren't you? Or has my darling ex-wife been telling you stories out of school?'

'Women talk. You know that.'

'Well, men don't,' he snapped. 'Certainly not about their personal lives. Stop prying into mine, Jade,' he warned. 'I don't like it. Stick to your own. I'm sure it's colourful enough to amuse you.'

'One day, Nathan, you'll believe me when I tell you I'm not the promiscuous little tart you seem to think I am.'

Again Nathan smiled. It projected scepticism with a capital S.

Suddenly, Jade could not wait for Nathan to leave Whitmore's. *And* Belleview. He was far too judgemental of her for her liking. She also had the awful feeling that Gemma would not be safe till he was way out of sight and out of mind. Yes, everything would be much better without him being around!

CHAPTER SEVEN

As NATHAN drove across the Harbour Bridge Jade realised she hadn't been into the head office at Whitmore's for ages—maybe two or three years—but she knew her father pretty well and she was sure nothing would have changed. Pops was not a man who liked change.

Whitmore Opals occupied half of the seventh floor of a conservative rather than glamorous office block, tucked in behind the taller larger flashier buildings that faced Circular Quay. There was no view worth looking at through Whitmore's windows, unless one wanted to inspect the backs of other buildings or windswept alleyways.

The reception area was presentable enough with black leather seating, bluish carpet and the inevitable rented pot-plants. The reception desk itself was functional, however, rather than showy, as was the woman who'd sat behind it for a dozen years or more. Moira had been hired for her superb secretarial skills, not her looks. Jade's father did not believe in putting glamorous blondes on the front desk whose only talents lay in answering the telephone in sing-song voices or smiling seductive smiles at visiting clients and sales reps.

The head of Whitmore's also didn't believe in wasting money on unnecessary staff or housing them in overly lavish accommodation. Management had reasonably plush offices, but none, other than Byron, had his own personal secretary—if one could call Moira that. The other executives shared the secretaries and typists who all resided in one large room with 'Administration' on the door.

All the other sections had similar open floor-plan accommodation. Exports, Accounts, Sales, Personnel and

Design were each housed in the one large room on either side of a central corridor, Design being the only section where individual workers were given the privacy of cubicles to help them create the quality pieces that were the hallmark of Whitmore Opals.

Some of the more individual designs were never duplicated or reproduced, though these were usually ones commissioned for a particular opal that Byron had bought. Neither did Whitmore's make doublets or triplets, which were thin slices of opals adhered to a black backing to make the opal look bigger and brighter, the triplets having a glass or crystal cap further to enlarge the opal's appearance. Whitmore's only used solid opals in their jewellery—an uncommercial and snobbish decision, Jade thought.

Doublets and triplets might not increase in value, but they could still look beautiful and brought pleasure to people who could not afford the much more expensive solids. People didn't always buy opals for investments, Jade reasoned sensibly. If she were running the company, Whitmore's would make a much wider range of opal jewellery. They could supply the cheaper items to souvenir and gift shops all over Australia as well as export them to similar shops overseas.

Yes, Whitmore's had become an old-fashioned, stodgy company in Jade's opinion. It was to be hoped that with the employing of a young marketing manager like Kyle change was at last on the way.

Nathan's car crawled off the bridge and along the already jammed city streets before turning down a narrow lane which was refreshingly empty, though bleak-looking. He whizzed along for half a block before abruptly turning down the well-disguised ramp that led into the basement car park. There, after a couple of neatly executed corners, he slid the Mercedes into a reserved spot alongside a silver-grey sedan.

'Can I have your parking place when you're gone?' Jade asked Nathan once he'd turned off the engine.

'Sorry,' he said. 'No can do. This is Byron's spot. Mine's already been allotted to your Mr Armstrong.' And he pointed to the Magna alongside.

'He's not my Mr Armstrong. Yet,' she added, more to irritate Nathan than any real desire to pursue the man. Jade was not one to set herself up for further humiliation or rejection, and Kyle had made it quite clear the other night that he was not interested in her in that way.

'In that case, soon you won't have to worry about a parking place,' Nathan returned drily. 'You'll be able to ride in with *him* on the necessary mornings.'

'Very funny,' Jade remarked, ignoring Nathan and swinging her long legs out of the car. Standing up, she eased the straight, rather short skirt back down over her hips then straightened her sheer black tights. Bending to peer into the car's side-mirror, she checked her make-up, readjusted her black and gold earrings, ruffled her blonde hair up on top and patted it down at the sides before last, but not least, moistening suddenly dry lips. Taking a deep breath, she slung the gold chain of her black patent handbag over her shoulder and strode round to join Nathan, who was standing there watching her with a sardonic expression on his face.

'The poor bastard,' he muttered, looking her up and down.

Jade might have shot back some suitably caustic comment but Nathan had already turned away to walk towards the basement lift where two more people were standing waiting. Neither of them was a Whitmore employee, since they didn't speak to Nathan, who remained silent during the ride up to the seventh floor. Jade did likewise, her nerves returning. Her mind was not on attracting Kyle, as Nathan might have thought, but on the job facing her.

What would her work consist of? Would she be able to make an intelligent contribution to the company? Would she make a fool of herself?

'Where have you put Kyle?' she asked once they stepped out of the lift and were alone in the corridor.

'In my old office. I've been occupying Byron's.'

'And where will I be located, do you know?'

'Kyle had another desk moved into his office yesterday.'

Jade did a double take. 'You mean I'm to be in the same room with him all day?'

Nathan ground to a halt outside the double glass doors that had 'Whitmore' in black lettering on one and 'Opals' on the other. 'Why the panic, Jade? That should surely play right into your hands. Nothing like being with a person constantly to create an atmosphere of intimacy. I would have thought you'd be ecstatic at the arrangement.'

'Do you know what, Nathan? You're getting to be a bore!' And, sweeping past him, she pushed the door open and marched inside.

Moira glanced up from Reception, managing to look both surprised and pleased at sighting Jade. 'Well, if it isn't little Jade, all grown up and very glamorous-looking. I almost didn't recognise you in that suit and with that blonde hair, but it suits you.'

'Thanks, Moira. You're looking well, too.'

The woman's smile was slightly sheepish. 'I have to admit it's been less harrowing working for Nathan here than your father. But I gather that situation will come to an end next Monday. Still, perhaps Mr Armstrong's arrival will take some of the load off Byron's shoulders and he'll be less stressed. What do you think, Nathan?'

'I think everyone might be in for a big surprise. A close brush with the grim reaper has a tendency to make one sit up and take stock of one's life. I wouldn't be surprised if Byron comes in here next Monday a changed man. You mark my words. I almost regret not being here to see it. I'll have coffee in ten minutes, Moira.' And, so saying, Nathan strode into Byron's office and closed the door behind him.

Both Moira and Jade stared after him, Moira in startled shock, Jade with dry scepticism.

Her father hadn't changed. Her father would never change. Black was still black in his eyes, just as white was white. Right was right and wrong was wrong. People were good or bad. There could be no grey. Except, of course, when it applied to his own private and personal life. Then things could be very grey indeed.

Moira cleared her throat and swivelled round in her chair to face Jade. 'That's telling us, isn't it? Still, Nathan's never been one to mince words.' Her face showed she admired him for that. 'So! You're going to be getting the feel of things by helping Mr Armstrong out a couple of days a week, Jade, is that right?'

'Uh-huh. He's a brave man, isn't he, taking on a troublemaker like me?' Jade was aware Moira probably knew all about the various problems she'd caused over the years. Byron had a tendency to talk very loud on the telephone when he was lecturing.

'A lot of teenagers go through a difficult time,' the woman said with sweet generosity, 'but you're all grown up now and very lovely, if I may say so.'

'Why, thanks, Moira, that's really sweet of you. Well, I suppose I'd better go and beard the lion in his den.'

'Jade, before you do, I just want to say I'm sorry about your mother and to apologise for not coming to the funeral. Someone had to hold the fort here and, to be honest, I never did get to know Mrs Whitmore very well. She didn't come to any of the staff functions and... well...'

'And she never invited any of the staff to Belleview,' Jade finished for her, hating the way she felt when she had to talk about her mother, not to mention the guilt that consumed her because she couldn't bring herself to feel grief or loss over her death. Regret was the closest to either she could summon up, regret that the woman had made it impossible for people to love her. 'It's all right, Moira,' she sighed. 'I understand.'

The door of Nathan's old office opened and Kyle stood there, staring over at her. His coldly black but strangely sensual gaze hit her between the eyes—and in the stomach—as forcefully as it had the first time. She gulped and tried telling herself he wasn't that good-looking, or that sexy, even if he *was* wearing a magnificent pale grey lounge suit which would have looked well on any man, let alone one as elegantly built and attractive as he was. Jade just barely stopped her own eyes from eating him up the way a hot, tired trucker might eye a cold frothy beer. He, of course, was surveying her back with his now familiar cool style, showing not the slightest hint of either the surprise or admiration Moira had afforded her, let alone any real interest or desire.

It quickly came to Jade that working closely with this man would take considerable control on her part. Still, she supposed she should be getting used to personal rejection by now!

Plastering a bright smile on her face, she walked towards him. 'Hi, there!' she greeted breezily. 'I'm here in good time. Look, it's only ten to nine.'

'So it is. You're going to be working in here,' he said. 'With me.'

'Yes, Nathan told me on the way in this morning.' Jade kept smiling as she brushed past him on her way into the office where immediately she saw that her desk had been placed at right-angles to his. She would be working even closer than she'd imagined. God!

She whirled round just as Kyle closed the door. 'Before I forget,' she said a little breathlessly, 'do you think one of those reserved parking spots in the basement could be arranged for me?'

'No,' he said bluntly, and strode over behind his desk. She followed to stand on the other side, facing him. 'Why not?'

His expression was so bland she felt like hitting him. 'It would cause trouble with other members of the general staff who don't have the privilege of a personal parking space. Only management has that perk, certainly not a part-time assistant.'

Jade frowned her instant disgruntlement. She was more than a part-time assistant, surely. One day she'd own the damned company. 'Surely, as Byron's daughter, I should be able to—'

'I don't believe in blatant nepotism,' he interrupted curtly, his face turning hard. 'A person should earn privileges, not have them handed to him—or her—on a silver platter.'

Jade felt her control slipping. 'If you don't believe in nepotism then why give me this job in the first place?' she snapped. 'If you did it just to suck up to my father then you pulled the wrong rein. My father doesn't believe in women holding executive positions. The only position he likes them in is the missionary position!'

Jade regretted this last comment the moment it slipped out of her mouth but to her surprise Kyle laughed. 'Let me assure you, Jade, I didn't hire you hoping to score brownie points with your father, though he may be grateful to me in the end. I saw qualities in you that perhaps your father is incapable of seeing with those undoubtedly biased eyes of his.'

'What qualities?' she challenged, highly sceptical of this seeming about-face. 'Name one.'

'Boldness.'

Now Jade laughed. 'You find boldness a quality? My father finds my boldness a pain in the butt.'

'I can appreciate that,' he admitted drily. 'But, as I've already pointed out, I am not your father.'

'Boldness, eh? Name another of these mysterious qualities of mine.'

His smile, when it came, took her breath away. Go back to your other face please, she wanted to tell him. I can almost cope with that one!

'I think you've had enough flattery for one morning,' he drawled. 'Let me just say I think your various qualities can translate into tangible assets for the marketing section of this ailing company, *provided* you can be stopped from going over the top. Your qualities need a firm hand, Jade. And direction.'

'And *you're* going to be my firm hand?' she mocked.

'I would prefer the word "director".'

'Then direct me to where I can park within walking distance of this place.'

'I said director, Jade, not babysitter. Find your own parking place. If you can't, then catch the train or the bus like everyone else. Or alternatively, ride in with your father. He'll be coming in from next Monday.'

Jade gritted her teeth and counted to ten. Underneath, she was grudgingly impressed by the man's stand—and almost pleased by his highly unexpected though rather backhanded compliments—but she'd be darned if she was going to give in without a fight.

'What about this Friday afternoon?' she argued. 'I'll be coming here straight from university. I can hardly leave my car behind.'

'Can't you catch a train that day?'

'I could, but my lectures don't finish till one. It would take me ages to get here by public transport in the middle of the day. By the time I arrived it would almost be time to go home again.'

'Not really, I always work late on a Friday and so will you as my assistant. But I'm not an unreasonable man. You can have my parking spot on Friday, *if* you agree to drive me home afterwards.'

Jade blinked. She hadn't expected him to capitulate. She certainly hadn't expected him to offer her his own spot. As for driving him home afterwards... Her heart fluttered wildly at the thought. Damn, but she'd resolved to ignore this unwanted desire, yet here she was, thinking all sorts of scandalous things.

'Where's home?' she asked, trying to sound casual while her insides were doing the fandango.

'Northbridge. Not that far out of your way.'

'It's a deal,' she said, knowing damned well she would have agreed even if he'd said the Blue Mountains. Or Timbuctoo.

'Right,' Kyle said brusquely. 'Now let's get to work. Do you like tea or coffee?'

Her eyes widened in surprise that he was offering to get *her* a drink, not the other way around. Clearly, he was no Nathan. 'Coffee,' she said. 'Black, no sugar.'

'Ah, yes, I remember now. Same as myself. Get yourself settled and start looking over the sales figures I put on your desk while I get the coffee. I won't be long.'

Jade's eyes followed him as he strode from the room, his walk elegant, the carriage of his head as arrogant as Nathan had said. But it was not an arrogance that grated, Jade realised. There was something eminently appealing about a man being as cool and self-possessed as Kyle was, who could stand up to the daughter of the boss one moment, then get her a cup of coffee the next. It came to her then that there was no chauvinism in Kyle Armstrong. God, but she liked that, she liked it a lot!

Shaking her head, Jade turned and walked over to the corner of the room where she hooked her handbag over a peg of the coatstand. The man was an enigma all right, not easily read. A man of mystery. So he liked her boldness, did he? Now that was a surprise! He certainly hadn't the other night. Still, that had been on a personal basis. Maybe it *was* an asset in marketing to be bold. A bold thinker might produce some new innovative daring strategies. Whitmore's could certainly do with them.

As for his declaration that she needed direction... Jade supposed he was right about that too. It was time to tone down her wild, tempestuous nature, high time to stop acting the rebel. Since she wasn't interested in embracing marriage and motherhood—lord preserve her from following her own mother's wonderful example—it was also time she put her head down and showed her father that she could make a real contribution to the family company, that she meant business!

Jade was still in front of the coatstand, smiling at her own pun when Kyle re-entered the room and threw her an exasperated glance.

'Something amusing you over in that corner?' he said curtly, kicking the door shut behind him and walking over to put a steaming mug on each desk. He glared down at the untouched sales reports. 'Don't tell me you haven't even sat down yet. Look, Jade, there's no room around here for any dead weight. You're either serious about this job or you aren't. I was hoping by your appearance this morning that you were!'

Jade bit her bottom lip and hurried over. 'I've never been more serious about anything in my life!' she pronounced. 'I'm sorry, Kyle. It won't happen again.'

'Make sure it doesn't. I've stuck my neck out hiring you, Jade. Don't make me look a fool.'

'I won't, Kyle. I'll be a model assistant from now on, I promise. I won't even breathe till I've read every single page here.' And she buried her face in the first report, not even touching the coffee.

'There's no need to get carried away,' he said drily.

The telephone on his desk rang then and he picked it up. Jade couldn't help but overhear his side of the conversation. After all, he was only a few feet away and the sales reports weren't *that* involving.

'Kyle Armstrong...'

A short tense silence was followed by a frustrated sigh.

'Look, I've told you not to ring me here. Couldn't this have waited till tonight?'

Jade's ears pricked up. One didn't need to be imaginative to get the drift. A girlfriend was making a nuisance of herself, ringing Kyle at the office when he'd told her not to. Despite her having suggested as much to Nathan, the thought of Kyle actually having a girlfriend brought an intense stab of jealousy. How dared he have a girlfriend? He'd hardly been in the state long enough to *meet* women, let alone snaffle one up for himself.

Oh, my God, she thought. Had he brought one with him over from Tasmania? A live-in kind?

I do not care! she told herself furiously. It means nothing to me. He's just my boss, nothing more. And a chauvinist after all, from the sounds of things. He's talking to that poor girl like dirt. I couldn't possibly fancy a chauvinist. I most definitely would not want to go to bed with one.

'I'll be home around nine,' he was saying sharply. 'Yes, do that, and don't—I repeat *don't*—ring me here again.'

He muttered something as he hung up. Jade looked up and their eyes met.

'Girl trouble?' she said between clenched teeth.

His gaze didn't waver but she could have sworn it turned a fraction smug. 'Something like that,' he drawled.

Jade's teeth clenched ever harder in her jaw.

I hate him, she decided once again.

CHAPTER EIGHT

JADE was still poring over sales reports and profits and loss statements when another mug of coffee materialised on her desk. Startled, she looked up to find Kyle standing there with a steaming mug in his own hand.

'It's gone eleven,' he said.

'Really?' she gasped, only then realising how absorbed she'd become in the figures. Absorbed and appalled.

'Yes, really,' Kyle said drily, and perched on the corner of her desk, sipping his coffee. 'Drink up. I'm sure you're in need of resuscitation after looking at those figures.'

She certainly was. 'I didn't realise things were that bad,' she said, and picked up her mug.

'Half of the problem is stagnation. The other half is Campbell Jewels, who have a stranglehold on the opal market, though it's not clear why. Admittedly, they undercut Whitmore's prices in their chain stores, but not in their duty-free shops around Sydney. In fact, their duty-free opal prices are actually dearer than Whitmore's. Yet their sales are still higher, a matter I'm investigating at the moment. Meanwhile, it might help if you tell me what happened between Celeste Campbell and your father to cause such a savage vendetta on Ms Campbell's part.'

Jade's shrug carried true confusion. 'I wish I knew. I think it goes back a long way.'

'Tell me what you do know.'

She did.

'Mmm. Since things settled down between the Campbells and Whitmores after your father's marriage to Irene Campbell, then something else had to have happened afterwards. Do you think there could have been

93

some personal involvement between Byron and Celeste around that time? An affair turned sour?'

'I have to admit that has crossed my mind,' Jade conceded. 'My parents' marriage was not a happy one.'

'Your father doesn't strike me as an adulterer, Jade,' Kyle commented thoughtfully.

'I'm sure he wouldn't be in normal circumstances,' she said, stunning herself with this new sudden insight. 'But my mother was...difficult to love.' Oh, Pops, she thought with an unexpected rush of emotion and understanding. Forgive me for taking such a holier-than-thou narrow-minded stand. We all need to be loved, and if we sometimes look for love in the wrong arms then who is to blame for that? Certainly not the unloved one.

Tears of remorse and something else stung her eyes, and she quickly dropped her lashes, hiding her distress as she sipped her coffee. A silence descended upon the room, Kyle seemingly giving her time to gather herself. Finally, she looked up, and those beautiful eyes of his were watching her closely, sympathy in their normally inscrutable black depths.

Sympathy was something Jade wasn't used to. For some reason, it annoyed her. Kyle's job was marketing, not probing into the private life of his employer.

'Now that I've had time to think about it,' she said sharply, 'I'm quite sure that's not the answer. Father would not do anything of the kind. He's an exceptionally moral man. Who knows? Maybe Celeste made a play for him and he turned her down. She's a real man-eater, that one. Though she usually prefers younger men. You'd better watch yourself, Kyle,' Jade flung at him a touch acidly. 'You'd be her type, and once she finds out you're working for us you'll become her prime target.'

His eyes glittered with dark amusement. 'How kind of you to warn me. But let me assure you, Jade, I'm not the sort of man who responds well to being a target of the opposite sex. *I* fire the bullets where women are concerned, not the other way around. That's the way mother nature made the beast, and that's the way I like it.'

Sliding off her desk, he walked over to the door where he glanced back over his shoulder at her, his mouth stopping just short of a smile. 'Excuse me for a moment,' he said with cool politeness. 'I have several things I wish to discuss with Nathan. Take a break till I get back, then we'll put our heads together and see what we can come up with to put Whitmore's back on the map.'

Jade sighed audibly once the door shut behind his exit. That man! He had a way of fascinating and irritating the death out of her at the same time. Had that been a slap on her wrist, the comment about *his* wanting to fire the bullets where the opposite sex was concerned?

As for putting their heads together...

Jade groaned as the image of Kyle kissing her flashed into her mind, bringing with it a definite curling of her stomach. Dear lord, never had a man affected her like this before. It was utterly, utterly amazing. And utterly, utterly futile. Kyle already had a female in town, panting for him so much that she had risked disobeying orders and ringing him at the office.

Jade frowned over that phone call for a moment. Kyle had been arrogant and quite rude to the person on the other end. Funny, she wouldn't have thought that was how he'd treat a woman-friend. She would have imagined him being a suave charmer, always doing and saying the right thing.

Damn, but he was really getting under her skin. Why was she getting the sickly feeling that there was something not right about him, something not quite real?

Something Nathan said in the car came back to haunt her, something about Kyle bearing close watching. What had he meant by that? Did he think there was a chance Kyle was some kind of industrial spy? A saboteur, maybe, from Campbell Jewels?

Her mind flashed back to that phone call. Maybe it wasn't a woman who'd called him. Or maybe it was? Could Kyle be already involved with Celeste Campbell? Was that the solution to all these niggling concerns?

It didn't seem possible. In fact, it was a crazy idea, Jade finally accepted. If he was Celeste's spy, he would not be asking questions about her, would he? She was becoming paranoid.

Jade was glad when she suddenly remembered her promise to Gemma to get in touch with Lenore about going shopping. Anything to distract her from that infernal man! After a quick dash to the ladies' room, she elicited Lenore's number from the highly efficient Moira and returned to her desk to dial. An answering machine told her that Lenore would be at the Drama Theatre at the Opera Hall all day rehearsing. Jade hung up, thinking she might walk over there during her lunch-hour. It wasn't far.

The door opened and Kyle came in, looking pensive. 'I hope,' he informed her with a worried look, 'that I haven't bitten off more than I can chew here.'

Jade was privately astonished that he would admit to any doubts about his abilities. Yet, in a way, his expressing even the smallest degree of apprehension came as a relief. This wasn't the action of a dastardly con-man, intent on inveigling his way into everyone's confidence in order to cause trouble for Whitmore's. Such a bounder would be all bluff, displaying not a chink in his armour.

Jade found herself warming again to Kyle. God, would she never stop this see-sawing of emotions where this man was concerned? Still, she much preferred liking him to hating him. Though both made her heart race like that of an adolescent schoolgirl.

'I have every confidence in you, Kyle,' she praised. 'After all, you can't do worse than Father has been doing. Besides,' she added with a cheeky grin, 'you have me by your side and that has to be worth something. Not much, perhaps, but I'm a trier. And bold, remember?'

Kyle blinked at her for a few moments before throwing his head back and laughing.

'I didn't think what I said was *that* funny,' she said stiffly, all the while trying not to stare at the man.

Laughing, Kyle was more devastatingly attractive than ever.

He flashed dazzling white teeth at her, his laughter slowly being reduced to a wide smile. 'You are the most entertaining female I have ever come across.'

Jade bristled. 'Is that why you hired me? To be your court jester?'

'No,' he said, his smile now a mere quirk at the corner of his mouth. 'Nothing could be further from the truth. My reasons for hiring you were deadly serious. So let's get to work, Ms Whitmore. We have a company to save!'

By two o'clock, Jade's head was reeling. What a taskmaster! What a slavedriver! She'd heard of *think* tanks. Well, she'd just drowned in one!

'Kyle,' she said at last when her stomach started grumbling. 'I'm awfully hungry.'

He glanced at his wristwatch, which, if she wasn't mistaken, was a most expensive one. Clearly, Kyle spent a good proportion of his salary on his personal appearance, if his clothes and accessories were anything to go by. His grey suit had 'Italian' written all over it. His white shirt was the finest lawn. And his dark red tie with the black dots and matching kerchief were silk. A diamond sparkled in the corner of the gold and ebony ring he was wearing on the middle finger of his right hand.

'I didn't realise it was so late,' he muttered. 'You should have said something earlier.'

'And stop our brilliant flow of ideas?'

His smile curled her stomach. 'They *were* pretty good, weren't they? You're right of course about starting a cheaper line of opals. That's only common sense. And I loved your idea of an annual ball with the belle of the ball being presented with a solid opal pendant. The free advertising that will get us from the society pages and women's magazines will be invaluable.'

'Well, I adored your idea of an auction at the ball,' Jade countered enthusiastically, 'not to mention Whitmore's sponsoring a major horse-race. That's what we desperately need. Some exciting promotion and exposure. Opals have too staid an image.'

'Whitmore's won't have too staid an image if *you* ever get your hands on the reins,' Kyle said drily.

'Do I take that as a compliment?'

'I'm sure you will.'

'Meaning?'

'Meaning I've never known a young woman to be as impregnable to criticism and disapproval as you are. Do you ever care what people think of you?'

Jade's laughter was slightly bitter. 'Oh, I see. You've been talking to Nathan about me. You know, Kyle,' she said, standing up and straightening her skirt, 'you shouldn't believe half of what people say about me. For one thing, I don't change my men-friends every other week at all.'

'Only every month or so?' he taunted as she walked over to get her handbag from the coat-stand.

She unhooked the bag before turning, her dark blue eyes flashing angrily. Was she to be plagued with male hypocrites for the rest of her life? Her smile was a cover for her fury.

'Every month?' She pretended to consider the concept seriously. 'Well, perhaps that is going too far. I doubt any of my relationships have lasted *that* long. I have to confess, Kyle, that I have a low boredom threshold when it comes to men. Once they show their true colours— and they invariably do—I quickly lose interest.' This she delivered while looking him straight in the eye.

'And what true colours are those?' he demanded to know, his voice clipped and hard.

'Oh, the usual,' she retorted airily.

'You mean they only want sex from you?'

She laughed. 'Don't be silly. That goes without saying. No, it's their need to control everything that drives me mad. Just because you go to bed with them, they think they can start running your life!'

'How naïve of them,' he drawled. 'Maybe some women can be controlled by gaining a sexual upper hand, but I would imagine that would never work with you,

Jade. A man would need a far greater lever when it came to capturing and holding *your* interest.' He smiled at her, a darkly cool and disturbingly enigmatic smile. 'Now hadn't you better toddle off for lunch? I want you sitting back at that desk no later than three.'

Jade stared back at him for a few electrically silent moments, her heart racing. Then she turned, and left the room, hating herself for allowing Kyle to continue to intrigue her. If she kept this up, next thing she knew she'd really fall in love with him. And that would never do.

Jade had once enjoyed playing at falling in love, but her recent experience with Nathan had taught her that really falling in love could bring considerable heartache. Creating a career for herself, she decided, was far more important than surrendering to an emotion fraught with such dangers. She wanted to succeed at Whitmore Opals, wanted quite desperately to show her father she could be as businesslike and successful as Nathan.

But she wouldn't do that if she started mooning over Kyle or going all gooey every time he threw a smile her way. No wonder men thought women had no place in business. Jade didn't doubt a lot of them let personal issues get in the way of their better judgement. Well, no more. From now on she would be all business. In fact, she would be as cool and controlled as Mr Cool himself!

The day had turned bleak and windy. Or was it just the narrow city street, sandwiched in between the tall buildings, blocking out the sun and forming a natural tunnel that accentuated any air movement? Whatever, Jade shivered as she hurried along, sighing her gratitude when turning the corner brought back the sunshine and no breeze at all.

The takeaway sandwich place she found a couple of doors along was empty. And why not? she thought tartly. It was no longer lunchtime!

With a salad sandwich, a low-fat chocolate milk drink and an apple in a paper bag, she strode quickly across the pedestrian crossing and into the quay area where there was no shortage of people dashing for trains and ferries.

Finding a spare seat in one of the harbourside parks, she devoured her sandwich and drink, refusing even to think about Kyle Armstrong. Much nicer to watch the ferries chugging into and away from the piers, or the other craft that was cruising the blue water of the harbour.

Her craving for food temporarily satisfied, Jade wandered down towards Bennelong Point and the Opera House. Synonymous with Sydney, it was a building you couldn't help but admire, but Jade decided she could well do without the myriad steps one had to mount to reach the front doors and foyer.

Having explained at Reception who she wanted to see, she was allowed to slip into the back of the theatre without any trouble. Rehearsal was in progress, with Lenore on stage. Jade sat down in the back row of seats and was soon absorbed in the play which was funny in both a witty and farcical way.

Jade loved the theatre, and went often, though she had always avoided Nathan's plays, after seeing one a few years back. It had been an emotive drama about family relationships, hitting too close to the bone for her taste. Jade wanted to be entertained when she went to the theatre, not put through an emotional wringer.

Her mind and eyes back on Lenore, she found herself admiring the woman's acting ability. She was quite brilliant and exquisitely beautiful as well. Jade envied her willowy elegance and that glorious red hair which was so vibrant under the spotlights. She could well understand Nathan not wanting a divorce from so desirable and lovely a woman.

When the group on stage abruptly broke off and Lenore moved down some side-steps and started walking down one of the aisles towards her, Jade was surprised. She was in shadow at the back of the theatre and would have thought Lenore couldn't possibly see her from the stage. Jade had been prepared to wait for a natural break in the rehearsal before letting her presence be known. All she could think was perhaps the lady who'd let her in had somehow got a message to Lenore.

Jade was about to stand and meet Lenore halfway when a dark figure did exactly that from a row of seats on the other side of the aisle. It was a man, Jade quickly realised, a tall well-built man with dark hair and wearing a dark suit. As he hurried towards Lenore, he came into better light and Jade's eyes rounded. *Zachary Marsden*? They widened even further when the couple clasped hands together like long-lost lovers and Zachary started swiftly to draw Lenore towards the back of the theatre.

'What is it, darling?' Lenore was saying as they approached the row where Jade was sitting like a statue. Impossible for them not to see her now that they were facing her way. No amount of shadow could hide Jade's white-blonde hair from that distance.

Lenore's gasp when she noticed Jade was full of shock and guilt. Jade herself was dumbstruck. Zachary was, after all, a married man with two children, a *happily* married man, she'd always thought. Jade's heart hardened towards this woman who'd always had her admiration and sympathy. Suddenly, she felt sorry for Nathan. So *this* was what had caused the divorce!

Lenore whispered something to Zachary, who threw Jade a worried glance before reluctantly leaving. Jade, at this point, still hadn't moved. Lenore came over and sat down next to her, sighing as she did so.

'Before you say a word,' she began immediately, 'this is not as bad as you think. Yes, I'm having an affair with Zachary, but no, it wasn't going on while I was married to Nathan. Zachary and his wife have agreed to divorce but they want to wait till their last boy, Clark, does his HSC exams at the end of this year. Not only that, Felicity was the one who asked for the divorce. She's fallen in love with another man.'

Jade stared at Lenore. 'Felicity? I don't believe it. She *adores* Zachary.'

Lenore shook her head. 'Felicity would always look as if she adored whatever man she was with. She's the clingy adoring type. But she certainly hasn't adored Zachary for quite some time, whereas I've loved him for years. Nathan and I were never in love, Jade. We only married because of Kirsty. I tried to make it work. Dear God, I tried for twelve long years, but Nathan...he...he should never have married at all. You know what he's like. He keeps all women at a distance. Emotionally, not sexually. He's mad about sex,' she finished with a caustic laugh.

'Yes,' Jade admitted drily. 'I can appreciate that.'

Lenore looked startled. 'Nathan hasn't been coming on to you, has he?'

Jade laughed. 'No, though I did throw myself at *him* once. It was quite interesting there for a minute or two but once he remembered who he was getting carried away with he stopped and gave me an enormous lecture. Sometimes, Lenore, I'm not sure what to make of Nathan. Is he a saint or sinner?'

'Maybe he's neither,' Lenore sighed. 'Maybe he's just human.'

Both women fell silent for a few seconds.

'You've met Gemma, haven't you, Lenore?' Jade resumed.

'Yes, I have. She's lovely, isn't she? I hope you're not here to tell me Nathan's seduced the poor girl already. Not that I didn't see it coming.'

'Oh? So he's been that obvious, has he?'

'Maybe not to everyone but certainly to me. You can't be married to a man as long as I was and not know the signs of sexual frustration.'

'He swears he isn't sleeping with her, you know. I tackled him about it this morning in the car on the way to work. Wednesday is one of my days in the office with that irritating Mr Armstrong I told you about on the telephone. Anyway, I don't want to talk about him— pompous man!—or Nathan for that matter. Believe it or not, I actually believed Nathan when he said he wasn't sleeping with Gemma.'

'I think it's just a question of time.'

'I couldn't agree more, which is why I'm here, Lenore. I've promised to take Gemma shopping tomorrow night at Chatswood to help her choose a working wardrobe and I was hoping you might come along, since you're so up on fashion. And I thought at the same time we both might drop a few hints about Nathan not being the right man for her, and...what are you laughing at?'

'Nothing much. Something just tickled my fancy. I can't tell you, I'm afraid. It concerns a little secret between your father and myself.'

Jade frowned. 'I hate secrets.'

'It's nothing to do with you, Jade. Truly.'

'If you say so. Well, will you come?'

'I'd love to.'

'Oh, goody. We'll have Gemma all glammed up and clued up at the same time. Look, I'd better fly. I have a feeling if I get back to the office even a minute late there'll be hell to pay. My boss alternates between being a new-age sensitive man and an even worse chauvinist than Pops, with the leaning towards the latter.'

'He sounds charming.'

'Oh, he is. That's the problem.'

Lenore's smile was wry. 'And good-looking?'

'Leaves Tom Cruise for dead.'

'You're not going to fall in love with him, are you, Jade?'

'Not if I can help it. The last thing I want is to stuff up this chance, Lenore. You know I've always wanted to learn the family business.'

'Yes, I know, but you have a habit of falling in love with the wrong man, don't you?'

Jade had to laugh. '*You* ought to talk.'

Lenore coloured guiltily. 'You won't tell anyone, will you, Jade?'

'Not a soul.'

'Thanks. I'd better go and call Zachary. He'll be worried. Now when and where shall we meet tomorrow night?'

Before they parted, Jade grabbed Lenore's hand, her face suddenly serious. 'I...I hope you'll be happy with Zachary, Lenore. I really do.'

There was a catch in her voice which squeezed at Lenore's heart. Happiness had been an elusive thing for Jade, she realised sadly. The girl tried so hard to be happy and outgoing all the time, but one didn't have to look far beneath the surface to find a troubled soul. The poor darling. If only she would stop flitting from boyfriend to boyfriend. If only she could find a good solid man like Zachary, a man of character and depth and sensitivity.

Too bad she was obviously attracted to this boss of hers. He didn't sound at all the right type for Jade. Besides, office romances could be very messy, especially with her being the boss's daughter.

A sudden thought came to Lenore and she grimaced. Dear lord, she hoped the new marketing manager at Whitmore's wasn't one of those cold ruthless bastards who'd do anything to get ahead. He wouldn't be the first good-looking man who thought he could either sleep or marry his way to the top. Maybe she should warn Jade.

And maybe I should just mind my own business, Lenore sighed. I have enough problems of my own.

CHAPTER NINE

AT PRECISELY one-thirty on the following Friday afternoon Jade zipped her natty white Ford Capri down the ramp of the basement car park, wondering if Kyle had remembered his promise to leave his reserved parking place empty for her, not to mention his condition that she drive him home later. She hadn't spoken to him since leaving the office at five the previous Wednesday. In fact, she'd had little opportunity to talk to him that afternoon at all after returning from her lunch break with Lenore.

Within minutes of her walking in the office door, Kyle had sent her out again to inspect their two retail outlets in Sydney with an eye to finding ways to update and improve their operation. She'd taken copious notes, her mind whirling with ideas to relate to him, but when she hurried back to work shortly before five Nathan had announced he was leaving straight away, if she wanted a lift home.

Kyle had seemed glad to see the back of her, she thought, and quite frankly she was at the end of her tether as well, both physically and emotionally. Some breathing space away from him would do her the world of good. She had been quite sure that, by Friday, she would have this unwanted reaction to his baffling sex appeal well and truly under control. Lust, she had found to her annoyance, was very distracting and not at all conducive to concentration. If she meant to succeed at Whitmore Opals, she would have to conquer it.

And the two days away from him seemed to have done the trick. She felt superbly composed and ready for the fray. She'd reorganised the notes she'd taken on Wednesday and couldn't wait to impress Kyle with her ideas. But her reaction to seeing the empty parking place quickly put a dent in her confidence. She started thinking about having to drive him home that night, and hoping he'd invite her in, hoping he'd . . .

Hoping he'd *what*? she berated herself sharply as she snapped off the engine. Make a pass at you? Take you to bed, even? As if he would. He doesn't even like you that way. Besides, he's already got a girlfriend. Why are you even *thinking* like this, damn you? Where is the new, cool, sophisticated, career-woman Jade?

She was smouldering with self-disgust by the time she reached the lift, folding her arms and standing in a corner for her ride up to the seventh floor. But, despite all her self-criticism, her mind would not let up on that rotten girlfriend.

Was she a live-in variety, or just a passing fancy? A sexual stop-gap, so to speak.

The lift doors shot open and Jade made her way out, walking slowly along to Whitmore Opals while she continued to torment herself over the relationship Kyle might have with his mystery girlfriend. It didn't seem likely any woman would have moved in with him so soon, not unless he *had* brought her over from Tasmania. But would a lover of such long standing tolerate the way he'd spoken to her on the telephone the other day? Jade didn't think so.

Still frowning, Jade pushed open the glass door.

Nathan, who was standing at the reception desk chatting to Moira, looked round immediately, his grey eyes cool upon her. 'I'd like to speak to you for a moment, Jade,' he said brusquely. 'Come into my office.'

'But . . . but . . .'

'I'm sure Kyle won't mind,' he said drily. 'Moira, contact Kyle on the intercom and tell him I've kidnapped his assistant for a few minutes, will you?'

Nathan waved Jade to a chair once he'd shut his office door but she declined, walking over to stand near one of the viewless windows.

'What do you want to talk to me about?' she asked impatiently.

'You and Gemma came home rather late last night,' he began as he sat down behind his large desk. Leaning backwards, he placed his elbows on the padded armrests, his long, elegant fingers linked in an arch in front of him. 'The shops closed at nine, yet it must have been eleven-thirty by the time you got in.'

'So?' she shrugged. 'We went for a drink afterwards. Is that a crime?'

'Gemma's not used to alcohol,' he said coldly. 'Or the sort of city dives you frequent. It's bad enough your changing the way she looks and dresses. Don't try to change the way she thinks and acts.'

Jade gave him a long, considering look. 'You know, Nathan, you keep claiming you have no ulterior motives where Gemma is concerned. And she certainly has been well briefed not to give anything away. So how come I continually get the feeling something is going on between you two?'

His smile carried too much cynical irony for Jade's peace of mind.

'What do you think of Gemma's new look?' she asked abruptly.

'I haven't seen Gemma since dinner last night.'

'Really? Well, you're in for a surprise.'

'A happy one, I hope.'

'That depends.'

'On what?'

'On what role you've cast yourself in where she is concerned. She looks really beautiful and a lot older. Very much a mature woman in every way.'

'And how large a hand did Lenore have in this transformation? I hope you didn't let her turn Gemma into a clone of herself. I asked you not to.'

'Why do you care?'

'I promised myself to look after the girl's welfare. I wouldn't like to see her spoiled. Or corrupted.'

Jade laughed. 'Then I suggest you look to yourself, darls, and not to me or your ex-wife. Lenore genuinely likes Gemma, as we all do, and she's just as concerned as I am over what stake you have in a girl of only twenty. You're thirty-five years old, a divorcee and a cynic. Gemma's a sweet innocent young thing who undoubtedly still believes in true love and marriage and playing happy families. Surely you can find other outlets for your male needs, brother dear, and leave her alone.'

Nathan glared at her for a moment, then grimaced. It was an odd expression for him, for it betrayed an inner turmoil that Jade found both bewildering and disturbing. Nathan was not given to moments of obvious emotional anguish. Anger, yes. And frustration. But not this black torment.

'I wish I could,' he muttered darkly.

Jade stared at him, horrified. 'Nathan, you *haven't*, have you?' Dear God, you lied to me the other day, didn't you?'

His cloudy grey gaze cleared to one of cold steel. 'I did not. Gemma is a lot safer with me,' he ground out, 'than she would be with a host of other men in this deplorable world.'

'Does...does she love you?'

'She thinks she does.'

Jade gasped her shock. Nathan's wording betrayed so much. 'And does she think you love her? No, don't answer that,' she rushed on, shuddering violently. 'I already know the answer. Oh, Nathan...you might not have seduced her body yet, but you've seduced her heart. She's far too young to know if she loves you or not. How could you be so wicked?'

He stiffened, his face hardening further. 'You don't know what real wickedness is,' he scorned. 'Besides, I certainly don't need you to lecture me on sexual morality. Or love, for that matter. You're the one who's always called any activity of your hormones "love". You claimed to be in love with me, remember? Am I to take it you've changed, along with your appearance? Poor Mr Armstrong,' he mocked. 'There I was, thinking you only lusted after him. If it's true love that has stirred your once fickle heart then I really pity him. You'll eat him alive!'

Jade felt an uncomfortable heat rushing through her, making her heart beat faster and turning her hands hot and clammy. 'I am not in love with Kyle Armstrong,' she denied fiercely. 'I hardly know the man.'

'You think falling in love takes time? Or knowledge of character?'

'Apparently not, since Gemma loves *you*,' she lashed out blindly before being overtaken with guilt and remorse. But pride, and a degree of confusion, had her chin lifting, her nose sniffing with indignation. 'I'm not going to stay here and trade insults. I have better things to do.'

She strode over and reefed open the door. 'And before you make some unsavoury crack,' she threw back at him, 'I'll have you know that any interest of mine in our new marketing manager is strictly business. I was only teasing you the other morning when I pretended to be after him. Do you honestly think a man like that would be my type? You'd have to be joking. I like my men to have blood in their veins, not ice!'

Head held high, Jade marched from the office, just managing to slam the door shut before she collided smack bang with Kyle Armstrong's very hard and surprisingly warm chest.

'Oh!' she cried out, blushing fiercely when he cupped her shoulders to steady her, all the while peering down into her highly flustered face. There was no doubt in Jade's mind that he must have heard every single word she'd just said. A swift glance over his shoulder revealed that Moira had temporarily deserted the desk, so at least there was no one else to witness her humiliation. Which was just as well, since she was practically dying from embarrassment.

'I...I didn't really mean any of that, Kyle,' she babbled. 'Nathan was needling me about you and I...I had to say something.'

God, but she wished he would let her go. He was so close and his hands felt so strong and all of a sudden her knees were going to water. This lust business was *hell*, she groaned silently.

'Which part didn't you mean?' he drawled.

'W...what?'

His hands fell from her shoulders back to his sides and she almost sighed aloud with relief. As it was she took a staggering step backwards, gulping when his cold black gaze drifted slowly down over her tailored red suit. It had a double-breasted jacket, the skirt straight and conservative in length. So how come his sardonic scrutiny made her feel she was wearing something highly erotic?

'Never mind,' he grated out. 'I take it you're now ready for some hard work?'

Jade somehow pulled herself together. 'Yes, of course.'

'Good. Because I'd hate to think you were just amusing yourself around here,' he snapped. 'I was talking to your father on the telephone earlier and I think you should know he's not expecting much from you. Quite frankly, Jade, no one seems to expect much from you.'

She sucked in a pained breath. Despite being no stranger to people's low expectations, they still hurt. Terribly.

'But I'm here to tell you that I do,' he stated sternly. 'I expect everything from you.'

'E-everything?' she stammered.

'Yes, everything. Dedication. Imagination. Inspiration. Perspiration. But above all, loyalty. I do not want to ever overhear you discussing your feelings for me, either personal or otherwise, with anyone else in this company, and that includes your brother. Because, in here, you're not Byron Whitmore's daughter, you're my assistant. Now get your butt into our office so we can get to work!'

So saying, Kyle took hold of Jade and gave her a propelling push along the corridor, landing a decisive smack on her bottom as she went. For a split-second she contemplated murder, but killing Kyle didn't seem worth twenty years' imprisonment, so she kept going, stomping along the corridor a few strides ahead of her rapidly following boss. There were many ways to skin a cat, she thought vengefully. Or freeze a Mr Cool!

But if Jade thought she was going to get away with giving Kyle the cold shoulder for the rest of Friday, then she was sadly mistaken. His formidable business hat now on, he brushed aside any feeble attempts of hers to make him suffer her frosty silence, jabbing at her pride by calling such tactics the childish display of a spoilt juvenile, as well as an easy cop-out because underneath she felt she couldn't make the grade as a real employee worth her salt.

In the end, stung by his insults, she was forced not only to speak, but actually to work with him.

By six, Whitmore's was deserted except for Kyle and Jade. At seven, he had a pizza delivered and Jade made their third batch of coffee. By eight they'd almost finished mapping out a comprehensive strategy to rescue Whitmore Opals. By nine, they had!

The hours had been long and hard, but oddly enough, Jade didn't feel at all exhausted. Exhilaration was closer to the mark. Not that she would ever admit such a thing to Kyle! But for the first time in her life another person had told Jade something she'd said or done was clever, that *she* was clever. Beneath her outer prickliness Jade was thrilled, her self-esteem soaring to new heights.

'I think we'll call it a night,' Kyle announced shortly after nine. 'Come next Wednesday you can start organising the ball, Jade. I'll have fixed up the sponsorship of the horse-race by then. I have connections with the Sydney Jockey Club. My main concern is getting that new cheaper line of jewellery into production and on the market. And I must remember to ask Byron if he has an opal that would be suitable for auctioning.'

'You could ask him about the Heart of Fire.'

'The Heart of Fire?'

'Yes, it's a large solid opal still in the rough that was stolen from Whitmore's many years ago but which turned up again recently.'

'How did it turn up?'

'You won't believe it. Some alcoholic old miner out at Lightning Ridge was accidently killed and his daughter found the opal in his belongings. She brought it to Sydney to us to have it valued, thinking she'd inherited a fortune, only to find it was stolen property. Now isn't that the most incredible story? Another interesting side-line . . . it's the same opal that is supposed to have caused the original feud between the Whitmores and the Campbells.'

'Mmm, that *is* interesting, but bad luck for the daughter. Do the police think her father was the thief?'

'I really don't know, but I doubt it. The opal disappeared on my father's and mother's wedding-day twenty-three years ago, during the reception at Belleview. It was in the safe in the library.'

'It's certainly a colourful story. And is it a very beautiful opal?'

'I've never seen it, but I'm told it is. It's supposed to be worth over a million.'

Kyle whistled. 'Such a story would get Whitmore's a lot of free publicity.'

'Oh, I doubt my father would sanction that,' Jade said quickly, worried that she might have spoken out of turn. 'He doesn't even like talking about that old feud within the family, let alone in public. Besides, the—er—miner's daughter has become a close family friend since coming to Sydney. We wouldn't want to embarrass her or hurt her feelings,' she went on, thinking to herself that the Whitmores had already caused Gemma more than enough heartache, with possibly more to come.

'It sounds as if you think highly of this girl, Jade.'

'Yes, Gemma is very sweet. Unlike me,' she added drily.

'You don't think you're sweet?'

She threw him a caustic look. 'Do you?'

Those black eyes glittered with a dry amusement as they looked her over. 'I've never liked sweet much. Give me spicy any time.'

Jade froze, her breathing suspended. Surely that was a flirtatious remark he'd just delivered? Surely he was looking at her with something approaching desire?

'Time for you to drive me home, I think,' he said brusquely, and looked away.

Jade stared at him while he stood up and turned to unhook his suit jacket from the back of the chair, her startled eyes riveted to the play of muscles beneath his shirt. She'd noticed, when he'd taken the jacket off hours earlier, what a nice body he had, that he didn't need false padding in his shoulders. But she'd been so annoyed with him at the time that any physical reaction to his male appeal had been blocked by anger. Now, with that disarming compliment just delivered, Jade found herself more than susceptible to the blinding sexual attraction that she'd felt for Kyle right from the first moment she'd seen him.

Her mouth was dry as she watched him shrug into the dark blue jacket. After pulling down his shirt cuffs and straightening his pale blue tie, he started to tidy his desk, throwing her a sharp look when she still hadn't moved.

'What's the matter? What are you still sitting there for? Surely you remembered to bring your car in, didn't you?'

'Yes,' she managed to get out, her dismay acute. She'd obviously been wrong about the desire in his eyes. *Very* wrong.

'Then what's the problem? I would have thought you'd have liked to get rid of me so that you could go out on the town. That's what most young people do on a Friday night, isn't it?'

His patronising tone propelled her out of the depression that was threatening. As did his indifference to what she did tonight after she dropped him off. She stood up and started clearing her desk with snappy movements, her reply just as snappy. 'Anyone would think you were old, the way you talk! You're only twenty-eight, for heaven's sake.'

When she looked up to glare at him, he was smiling over at her. 'Someone's been peeking at my résumé.'

'So?' she scoffed, doing her best to ignore her guilty colour. 'I was curious. What's wrong with that?'

'Absolutely nothing. Don't be so defensive. I'm flattered.'

'Don't be.'

His smile widened, if anything. 'All right, I won't. Now, can we go home?'

'We aren't going home,' she snapped. '*You're* going home.'

His smile faded. 'Meaning?'

'Meaning I'm glad you reminded me that young people go out on the town on a Friday night. Because after the week I've had I could certainly do with some relaxing.'

'You shouldn't drink and drive, you know,' he warned.

'Who said anything about drinking? I don't *drink* to relax, Kyle. Perhaps you'd like to ask me what I do do?' she taunted, knowing that she was being outrageous but unable to stop. Kyle certainly brought out the worst in her.

His face became a stony mask. 'I don't think so. I too have had enough for one week. Now get your keys,' he bit out.

'Say please.'

He simply stared at her, disbelieving of her defiance. Her chin tilted upwards and she smiled at him. Boldly. Irreverently. 'Go on. It won't kill you.'

Suddenly, he smiled back, a most peculiar smile that sent the hairs standing up on the back of her neck.

'All right, Jade. You win. *Please* get your keys and take me home.'

CHAPTER TEN

'I CAN'T get over how much different Gemma looks with her new hairstyle,' Ava commented towards the end of dinner that Friday night. 'That feather-cut around your face is so flattering, dear, yet your hair's still lovely and long. You'll have to get the name of the hairdresser for me from Lenore. I'm fed up with this frizz of mine.'

Gemma tried to smile at Ava's compliments, but Nathan's continued silence over her new look had already spoiled any pleasure the previous night's makeover and shopping spree had given her. Personally, she'd been *thrilled* with the co-ordinated wardrobe of skirts, trousers, jackets and blouses that Lenore had chosen for her in creams and tans and greens, even if it had cost a small fortune. But since she knew she was marrying Nathan the outlay seemed worth it. After all, she wanted him to be proud to present her as his wife, which he could do now. She no longer looked like a country bumpkin, but a smart sophisticated woman.

Lenore had shown her not only how to mix and match the various items, but also how to make up her face in a way complementary to both her new clothes and hairstyle. Tonight, she'd chosen to wear tan trousers and a cream cashmere sweater, the evenings having turned cool this past week. Her dark brown eyes were enhanced by subtle eye make-up in natural and brown tonings, her full lips glossed with a deep bronze lipstick. She'd shampooed and dried her thick brown hair, amazed and pleased when it simply fell into place around her face and shoulders. Clearly, the outrageous price charged for her haircut had been worth it!

The mirror in her room had told her she looked good before she came downstairs for dinner. So why didn't Nathan like her new appearance? Everyone else did, even

Byron. In fact, he'd fairly gushed over her, saying she looked utterly scrumptious and very grown up. Even when she tried not to take the credit, explaining that it had only been achieved with Jade's and Lenore's help, he'd still been very sweet.

'They had good material to work with, my dear,' he'd said warmly. 'Excellent, in fact. You were wise to take Lenore along with you. The woman has a splendid eye for fashion. Jade's my daughter and I love her but her taste is sometimes questionable, though there has been some improvement lately, I'm thankful to say. Though I think Lenore had a hand in that as well. I must ring her and thank her.'

Yes, everyone had said nice things earlier that day.

But not Nathan, who from the moment he'd arrived home from work this evening had been taciturn and obviously disapproving. Not that he'd actually said anything. He'd been annoyingly silent on the matter. But she'd caught him looking at her a few times and he hadn't looked too happy.

'What do you think, Nathan?' Ava said abruptly, and Gemma's eyes snapped to the man she loved more than life itself.

'About what?'

'About Gemma's hair, of course. Are you being obtuse or just plain difficult to get along with?'

Gemma waited for his answer with bated breath. Slowly, those beautiful grey eyes eyed her across the table, their scrutiny brief and cold. 'I'm sure it is very stylish, but I've always thought Gemma's face and hair were beyond compare. How can one improve on perfection?'

Everyone stared at Nathan, even Melanie, who was topping up Byron's coffee-cup at the time. Gemma began blushing, thankful that Kirsty wasn't present. Nathan's daughter was staying at a girlfriend's that night. Lord knew what the girl would have made of her father's saying such a thing to her.

Byron, Gemma noticed, was surprised though not displeased. Melanie was startled but Ava was looking almost bewildered.

Nathan chose that moment to wipe his mouth with his serviette and get to his feet. 'That was a great dinner, Melanie,' he said smoothly. 'But then your cooking is always superb. Please excuse me, everyone, I have some pressing personal business I must attend to.'

He strode from the room, his walk as elegant as his person. Gemma's eyes clung to his back till he disappeared.

'Nathan's in an odd mood tonight, isn't he?' Ava mused. 'From brooding silence to extravagant compliments to an abrupt disappearance all within seconds.'

'He's not an easy man to understand,' Byron admitted. 'But he's not given to idle flattery.' This with a close look Gemma's way. Ava began looking at her as well, a speculative expression on her face.

She busied herself sipping the last of her coffee.

'Well, he certainly made *me* feel good about my cooking,' Melanie said. 'I spent hours on dinner tonight. What was the general verdict? Is beef Wellington to have a regular appearance on the menu this winter?'

'*Winter*?' Byron growled. 'It's only autumn.'

'Same thing in my book. My cooking is divided into summer dishes and winter dishes.'

'It was delicious,' Ava said. 'I'll vote for it.'

'Yes, indeed,' Gemma agreed, grateful for the change of subject. 'Though I think the same as Nathan—all your cooking is superb.'

'I see we have two flatterers in the house,' Melanie said, smiling wryly.

Gemma felt her woman's heart stir with pity for the housekeeper, who, even when smiling, still looked incredibly sad. She was a lovely-looking woman but what kind of life was she leading, keeping house for a family not her own, and having no social life whatsoever except for a weekly visit to her brother? Would she never get over the tragic deaths of her husband and baby, and embrace love and marriage again? In ten years she would

be forty, then fifty, then sixty... Gemma wished Melanie
would make the choice to try life again, but she couldn't
see that happening while she hid herself away in Belleview, never meeting new people, especially eligible men.

Gemma stood up and started clearing the table.
Melanie let her do this nightly chore nowadays without
protest, knowing Gemma would do it anyway. Ava raced
away to catch the Friday night movie on television and
Byron took himself off to the library to read. He was
moving around a lot better, though still with the help of
a cane. Gemma could see the improvement in both his
leg and his temperament, though Kirsty was still threatening to go home to live with her mother, mainly because Byron refused to let her watch the soaps on
television on school nights.

Gemma suspected that was the reason for her staying
the night at her girlfriend's house. Nathan was going to
pick up both girls in the morning and take them to Avoca
for the weekend. Gemma, knowing she wouldn't be able
to resist Nathan's sexual advances in the setting of his
initial seduction, had declined to accompany them, much
to Nathan's obvious irritation.

Was that why he was in a mood tonight? Gemma
wondered as she went about the clearing up. It couldn't
be his finishing up at Whitmore's. He'd told her a few
times already that he wanted nothing more than to write
full time, and would be glad to see the end of working
in an office. He'd only stayed on out of gratitude to
Byron, not because he either wanted to or needed the
money. Gemma assumed he meant by this that he was
earning a good living from his plays.

They hadn't discussed money, as such. Or where they
would live after they were married, she realised with a
frown. Or children...

They hadn't discussed much at all, really.

Gemma was gnawing at her bottom lip as she stacked
the plates in the dishwasher.

'Did you get that letter that came for you, Gemma?'
Melanie said on joining her with a pile of cutlery. 'I put
it on your dressing-table.'

'No, I must have missed it. I wonder who could be writing to me here?'

'I think it's from your old lady-friend out at Lightning Ridge.'

'Ma?' Gemma was astonished. 'I only got a letter from her on Tuesday. I wonder what prompted another one. She hates writing letters.'

''Why don't you pop upstairs and read it? I'll finish this.'

'Thanks, Melanie. I'll do that.'

Gemma hurried upstairs, curious and pleased. She would never have dreamt she would ever be homesick for Lightning Ridge, and she certainly wasn't for the way of life. What young woman could prefer living in a primitive dugout in hot dry outback conditions to her existence in this beautiful Sydney home with its luxurious privacy and swimming-pool and lovely gardens?

But she did miss the feeling of belonging. No matter how nice everyone at Belleview was to her, she didn't really belong here. This was not her family. Her family—what she'd known of it—was buried in Lightning Ridge. So was her dog, Blue, who'd been her best friend.

She still missed Blue very much. And she missed Ma. Gemma was only now appreciating how kind Ma had been to her over the years. How many times had the old lady saved her from her father's foul temper? How many times had she lied for her, protected her, soothed her? Not only that, she gave good solid advice, full of homespun philosophy but not in any way old-fashioned. Ma was a realist.

Gemma hurried into her bedroom and snatched up the letter, ripping it open and sitting down on the side of her bed to read the contents.

Dear Gemma, Just a short note to let you know a man's been around asking questions about you and your dad. He said he was doing some Government census survey but I didn't believe him for a moment. He's one of them private eyes, I'll bet. He was specially interested about when you both came to live here but of course I didn't tell him anything. Anyway, I sent

him off to Mr Gunther who was the closest thing your
dad had to a friend around here. I hope I did the right
thing. By the way, you didn't say anything about
Nathan Whitmore in your last letter. Is that good news
or bad? You don't have to worry about shocking me,
love. Old Ma ain't shockable. Write soon and give me
the drum. And fancy you learning Japanese and going
to work in one of Byron's opal shops. I'm real proud
of you, love. Write soon. I sure love getting your
letters.

Your old mate, Ma.

Gemma folded the letter, a deep frown on her face.
'Trouble?'

Startled, Gemma's head whipped round to see Nathan
standing near the open doorway, looking as impossibly
handsome as ever. The light from the chandelier above
was giving his flaxen hair a softly golden glow. He'd
also abandoned the business suit he'd worn at dinner for
casual beige trousers and a cool green silk shirt which
was open at the neck. A thin gold chain lay around that
neck, drawing her eyes to the smooth tanned V on
display.

Before she could answer his query, he walked in,
shutting the door behind him.

Gemma swallowed. The physical chemistry between
them was so strong that just being in the same room
with him was agitating, even with other people present.
Being alone with him in the bedroom was murder.

'Ma says a man's been asking questions about me
around Lightning Ridge,' she blurted out, jumping to
her feet. Fortunately, Nathan stopped his advance at the
foot of her bed, his right hand curving over one of the
ceramic bed-knobs that decorated the brass bed. Relieved, Gemma sat back down on the side of the bed. 'I
suppose that's the man you hired?'

'I guess so. I instructed Zachary to handle the matter
for me.'

'Zachary?'

'Zachary is the Whitmores' solicitor. Among other
things,' he muttered.

'Oh. Has... has he found out anything concrete yet?' Gemma didn't like to get her hopes up about finding her mother alive, or even contacting her mother's family. But it was hard not to.

'No. Zachary said with so little to go on it could take months.'

Gemma's frown returned. 'That will cost an awful lot of money...'

When Nathan came round to sit beside her on the bed, taking her hands in his, she froze inside. Dear lord, if he started kissing her, she would have no hope of keeping to her resolve not to sleep with him again till they were married. He'd been fairly good about her decision to save further lovemaking for their wedding-night, but Gemma suspected that, underneath, he was as intensely frustrated as she was. She shivered when she recalled what a virile man he was, and how often he could make love in one night, not to mention the ecstasy she felt when he was doing so. But the urge to make him prove his love, to ensure that he *did* marry her, was almost as strong as her desire to be in his arms once more.

Only *almost*, however. He could tip the scales in his favour very easily, she suspected.

'I think there's something you should know about me, Gemma,' he said softly, 'and then I won't have to hear any more nonsense about money. I am a very rich man, my wealth totally independent of my adopted family. My maternal grandparents made me their heir and I inherited a considerable private income a few years back. I do not have to work. I do not have to write plays. If I wished, I could spend my entire waking life doing nothing but make love to you...'

Gemma tried to draw her hands away from his suddenly tightening grasp but his hands were like steel traps and for some unaccountable reason his refusal to let her go frightened her. When his mouth started to descend towards hers, her head jerked back. 'No, Nathan, don't!' she cried. 'Please... you promised.'

He eyed her with a small, dry smile. 'What did I promise? Only that I wouldn't sleep with you again before our marriage. Does that mean I can't even *kiss* my fiancée? Which reminds me...' Letting her hands go, he drew a wine-coloured velvet box from his trousers pocket and snapped it open, showing her the most magnificent solitaire diamond engagement ring.

She simply stared for several seconds, before lifting blurred eyes to his. 'Oh, Nathan... It's so beautiful...'

'Not beautiful enough,' he said, 'for my extremely beautiful lady.'

She took the box and dropped her eyes back to the diamond, rubbing a fingertip over the sparkling gem, a lump in her throat. 'I... didn't think you thought me beautiful any more when you came home tonight,' she murmured.

He sighed and tipped her chin up till she was looking into rueful grey eyes. 'I acted like a jealous fool,' he admitted. 'And I apologise. Of course you look beautiful, so beautiful that it's killing me not to kiss you and touch you. God, Gemma,' he groaned, and before she could do a thing he was crushing her to him, his mouth feasting on hers like a starving man. She couldn't help but respond, her heart and body leaping. But when he bent her sideways on to the bed and his hands began a fevered journey down her back, she started struggling. When she dropped the ring box and it rolled off her lap on to the floor, she cried out in dismay.

'My ring!' she wailed.

They sat up, both breathing heavily.

'I'll find it,' Nathan offered resignedly, dropping down on to his knees and sweeping the floor with his hands till he found it. 'Here it is. I guess we'd better check to see if it fits, not that you can wear it openly as yet. But I thought you might like a ring as a token of my commitment and love.'

A strangled sob broke from Gemma's throat. 'You make me feel awful.'

'Not as awful as I'm feeling at this moment.' He laughed before picking up her left hand and sliding the ring on her ring finger.

It was a little too large.

'Oh, what a pity,' Gemma murmured, content to stare down at her hand. The whole incident had really upset her, mostly because she really wanted to give in to Nathan. His giving her the ring should have reassured her of his love, but still her trust lacked something. Maybe everyone around Belleview was to blame with their warnings and their innuendoes about him. Maybe her own past had set up a basic mistrust of the male sex. Her father had been a cruel, hard man. Then there was that other awful time when another miner had sexually assaulted her. That *must* have dented her faith in men, even if she wasn't consciously aware of it.

'I'll have it made a size smaller,' Nathan said, putting the ring back, snapping the box shut and slipping it back into his pocket. His eyes ran over her mouth, a dark passion reflected in their gaze. 'I presume there's no chance of starting up where we left off?'

'I . . . I'd rather not . . .'

'That sounds wonderfully indecisive. Are you saying you could be persuaded?'

Gemma's chin shot up. 'I've no doubt you could persuade me into just about anything, Nathan, as you very well know. But if you love me, please don't try.'

She flinched when his hand reached out to trace a highly tantalising fingertip along her jawline, around her mouth then down her neck to linger on the pulse at the base of her throat. His eyes, narrowed and hard now, remained on her parted lips, her rapid breathing betraying her already dangerous state of arousal.

'I'm glad to see that the fancy hairstyle and clothes haven't changed the girl you are,' he said in a low, husky voice, 'but once we're married there'll be no more of these testing games. You will let me make love to you whenever I want.

'Don't worry . . .' That tantalising hand travelled down to where her breasts were pressing their swollen contours against the soft cashmere of her new cream sweater. Slowly and insidiously, with a strangely mesmerising rhythm, he played with her right breast, all the while talking to her in a calm, extremely hypnotic voice. 'You

won't find my demands any hardship, my beautiful
Gemma, because I aim to love you as no woman has
ever been loved before. We will be so finely attuned, you
and I, that when you see me looking at you a certain
way your body will automatically respond. We'll be one
as no two people have ever been one and you'll never
want any other man. Of course, if you ever so much as
look at another man, I might strangle you with my bare
hands...'

He bent to press feathery lips to hers, his hand returning to her throat where it slid around its slenderness
in what might have been a threatening gesture, if Gemma
had been capable of feeling threatened at that moment.
She was, however, totally enthralled, her body revved to
a state of high sexual excitement, her dazed mind eager
for what sounded like a relationship so intimate and
fiercely loving that she could hardly wait.

When his head lifted, she swayed towards him, lips
parted, heart pounding. 'Nathan... Oh, Nathan...'

He kissed her once more, a deep drowning kiss that
demonstrated his power to reduce her will-power to water
in no time flat. But then he put her aside, a dark mocking
smile on his mouth. 'This next four weeks is going to
be hell,' he rasped. 'But, oddly enough, I have to agree
with you. It will be much better all round if we deny
ourselves till we're legally joined. You'll feel much more
secure then, and much more willing to surrender yourself
totally to my love.'

He left her then, left her to suffer as she had never
suffered before, left her to lie down on her bed, wide-
eyed and aching for him. She tossed and turned, her
need to totally surrender herself to his love already a
tangible thing that tormented her body with a rest-
lessness just short of screaming point. She wanted to go
to him and tell him she'd changed her mind about going
to Avoca with him this weekend, about a lot of things.
She wanted to beg him to put her out of her misery.

But some inner instinct told her Nathan would not
change *his* mind again. The moment for savouring his

lovemaking had passed. She had rejected him one time
too many and the offer had been withdrawn.

Four weeks, she groaned.

It seemed an eternity away.

CHAPTER ELEVEN

'TURN right at the next set of lights,' Kyle said.

Jade did not reply, just did as he instructed, her mind still on that peculiar smile he'd delivered back at the office while saying she had won. Won what? His meekly saying please? That was a laugh! She had seen the mocking behind the pretended meekness. As well as the arrogance. Kyle Armstrong would never be a yes-man. So what had he meant?

'Pull over,' he said abruptly, startling her out of her reverie.

'Here?' she queried, guiding the car into the kerb outside an all-night chemist.

'Yes. I have to buy something,' he said, opening the passenger door and climbing out almost before she'd cut the engine.

He was back in less than a minute, a small paper parcel in his hand. She declined showing any curiosity over what he'd bought and he declined telling her, merely slid back into the car and snapped his seatbelt back into place. 'Turn left at the next intersection,' he ordered, 'then second on the right which will take you down to a small bay. Home's not far from there.'

After checking the oncoming traffic, she pulled away from the kerb.

'You drive well,' he complimented as she swung round the corner, as per instructions.

'Thank you,' she murmured, trying not to sound as ridiculously pleased as she felt. But compliments did not come Jade's way very often. At least, not about anything other than her looks and her body.

And she *was* a good driver—if a little too fast sometimes. She certainly had to brake sharply when the road suddenly dropped down a steep incline. 'Sorry,' she muttered, then stayed silent, having to concentrate on the narrow, curving road that was taking them down to the small bay Kyle had mentioned.

'Where to now?' she said, finally having reached the bottom of the hill where the road flattened to run alongside the edge of the cove. It was a very pretty place, with a small marina housing various crafts and a line of trees between the road and the shore.

'Just pull in here,' Kyle said, and pointed to a small parking bay beside a long wooden pier that stretched a fair way out into the water. At the end of it sat what looked like a permanently moored houseboat. It seemed far too big to be the kind that put-putted around the harbour.

'That's where I'm living at the moment,' he said, seeing the direction of her eyes.

'In that houseboat?' She was astonished. Such a dwelling didn't come cheap, especially in this area of Sydney. Middle Harbour and its surrounds were top drawer.

'It belongs to a friend,' he explained before she could ask.

The penny dropped immediately. He had a rich girl-friend, a *very* rich girlfriend.

'No,' he said drily. 'A male friend.'

Irritated by his mind-reading ability, she threw him a caustic look. 'Did I say anything?'

'You didn't have to. Your face is an open book.'

'Is it, now?'

'Yes,' he said, and laughed. She didn't like the sound of that laugh. It was far too arrogant and far too knowing.

When he went to get out and she didn't, he slanted sardonic eyes back over his shoulder. 'Don't you want to come in?'

'Not particularly.'

He sighed and slid his legs back into the car, slamming the door shut again. Now his eyes carried exasperation. 'I know women are contrary by nature but honestly, Jade...'

'Honestly what?'

'God,' he muttered, and, twisting abruptly in his seat, he reached over, snapped off her seatbelt then slid a cool firm hand around the back of her neck, turning her to face him. Jade was so stunned that she simply stared at him, her lips slightly parted in shock.

'That's better,' he rasped, his gaze dropping to her mouth. 'Oh, yes, that's much better...'

His fingers tightened around her neck and he pulled her ever so slowly closer, his own body shifting forward so that their mouths were destined to meet over the gearstick.

Jade's heart was thudding madly in her chest by the time his lips actually made contact with hers, her blood roaring, her head whirling. He was going to kiss her, she thought dazedly. Kyle was going to kiss her. Kyle *was* kissing her. Oh, God...

She moaned softly deep in her throat and his fingers tightened further, biting as deep into her flesh as his tongue was sliding deep into her mouth. Both her hands fluttered up to rest against his shirt and she could feel his own heart slamming against his chest wall.

I've died, she thought. Died and gone to heaven.

Suddenly heaven vanished, and she was back in the real world, Kyle's mouth deserting hers. Automatically, she straightened to sag back into her seat, but her wide eyes never left his. He was shaking his head at her and smiling that peculiar smile again, although this time she thought she understood it better. It was self-mocking.

'I was right,' he said cryptically, and not that happily. 'Damn and blast. Who would have believed it?'

'Right?' she repeated blankly. 'About what?'

He took both her hands in his and lifted them to his lips. 'You do want me, don't you, Jade?'

He was kissing her fingertips and she could hardly think. 'I...I...'

'Why can't you say it? You got your message across loud and clear last Saturday night. Don't be coy now, Jade. That's not your style. Say it,' he rasped, yanking her over so close that her panting breath was mingling with his. 'Tell me you want me,' he urged huskily. 'Tell me you've been wanting me all week. Tell me *I'm* the man you want to relax with tonight.'

His hot, erotic words had set her head reeling and her blood on fire.

'Say it, damn you! I want to hear you say it!'

'I...I want you,' she blurted out. 'Want you,' she moaned as his mouth fused with hers.

Jade had been kissed many times in her life before but never like this. She trembled beneath his devouring lips, his fiercely demanding tongue. Trembled and moaned.

Both of them were panting raggedly when Kyle finally brought the kiss to an end. 'Glad to see you won't disappoint me, Jade,' he said ruefully. 'This is not what I intended, you know. But I can't fight you—or your body—any longer.'

He flicked open the top two buttons of her jacket and slid a surprisingly cool hand inside, caressing a single taut breast, making her gasp when he started rolling the nipple around in his fingers, bringing it to a peak of such exquisite arousal that she cried out.

'How responsive you are,' he muttered thickly, then, quite abruptly, withdrew his hand and did up the buttons. 'But enough of that for now. A car is hardly the place to adequately pursue our mutual desires. I'm sure you gave up such adolescent activities years ago, as did I. There is a perfectly comfortable bed inside the houseboat, as well as champagne, music and other mod cons. Let's adjourn, shall we, and take advantage of them?'

He was out of the car in a flash and coming around to open her door, which was just as well since she was sitting there in a rather dazed state. When he reefed the door open and shot a hand down to help her out, she stared up at him. My God, was that her Mr Cool, peering down at her with eyes like hot black coals? This was another man, a roused impassioned creature who wanted her maybe more than she wanted him, who would not be denied.

She placed a quivering hand in his and allowed him to draw her forth from the car, allowed him to draw her body hard and close against his so that she could feel his need. Groaning, he cupped her head and kissed her briefly again before dragging his mouth away with a dark laugh. 'You'll be thinking I haven't had a woman in years if I keep this up. Not true, I assure you. But I have to admit I haven't had too many quite like you, Jade. Come...'

He started hauling her along the pier, walking so fast that Jade had trouble keeping up on the uneven planked surface. Kyle's kisses and caresses had brought her to a pitch of arousal she'd never known before and while she longed to have him really make love to her—dear lord, hadn't that thought tormented her since meeting him?—alongside the desire lay a churning feeling of panic.

For when it came down to the reality of real sex, when the kisses were left behind and the nitty-gritty begun, she was hopeless, absolutely hopeless. Kyle was in for a big disappointment.

Jade had never worried about such inadequacies before. It hadn't been necessary because she hadn't cared. Her two fumbling teenager lovers hadn't commented on her lack of enthusiasm or expertise. They'd been only too happy to find a pretty and willing female, and hadn't given ratings as long as the desired end was reached. Her only other experience had been with that man after Nathan had rejected her and quite frankly she'd been too intoxicated to remember much of it. But she suspected she hadn't set the world on fire with her technique.

Yet Kyle seemed to expect her to set him on fire with her technique. The way he'd spoken about her—as though she was a right raver—was both unnerving and dismaying. My God, he probably thought she was a slut, just like Nathan had!

The pain of such a thought ground her to a halt. When her hand ripped out of Kyle's he swung round, almost glaring at her.

'What is it now?'

'I can't,' she choked out.

Kyle's fury was of the speechless variety.

'You don't understand,' she went on, her voice shaking. 'I . . . I haven't done this sort of thing nearly as much as you—and everyone else—seem to think. And I just can't . . . can't go to bed with you, especially with you thinking I'm nothing but a . . . a . . .'

She couldn't say it, her eyes dropping to the pier as a wave of shame hit her. For honestly, what had she expected him to think with the way she'd dressed and acted last Saturday night, not to mention the outrageous things she'd said all week about her men friends and such? If he thought she was cheap and easy then she damn well deserved it!

A firm finger tipped up her chin and Kyle was looking at her with a dark frown on his face. 'How often is not often?' he said. 'You said you changed lovers at least once a month.'

Her blush was fierce, her mortification acute. She wished she could go back and cut her tongue out. 'I . . . I was exaggerating.'

'OK, I can accept that. Then give me a ball-park figure. Approximately how many lovers *have* you had? Five? Ten? Fifty?'

'I don't have to approximate,' she muttered, her eyes dropping again. 'I know the exact number. It's three.'

The silence was electric and she didn't dare to look at him for fear of seeing his scornful disbelief. 'I'm not lying,' she insisted shakily. 'The first two were when I was a very silly mixed-up teenager. The other was a one-night stand a few months ago when I was . . . unhappy.'

Finally, she felt compelled to look up, only to find that Kyle was no longer facing her. He had turned away and was staring out over the water.

'Kyle?' She reached out and touched him lightly on the arm. 'You do believe me, don't you? I'm not lying, I swear.'

His face was totally unreadable as he turned to gaze down at her. 'Have you always used protection when you had sex?'

'Yes, always.'

'And have you ever enjoyed sex with a man, Jade?'

She didn't know what to say. She'd enjoyed Nathan kissing her, but surely that was not what Kyle meant.

'Tell me,' he ground out. 'I need to know.'

'Not really,' she admitted. 'But I...I'm sure I will with you,' she added, fearful now that *he* would be the one to back out of tonight. Suddenly, she didn't want that. She wanted...oh, she didn't know what she wanted any more, except that she wanted him to keep on wanting her the way he'd wanted her a minute ago.

But maybe he'd only been wanting her because he thought she was a woman of experience, she realised wretchedly. Someone who knew all the sexual tricks, who could pleasure him in sophisticated ways unknown to her, who wouldn't be hesitant or nervous or just plain stupid.

No, no, I'm not stupid, she denied fiercely to herself. I'm not, I'm not!

Tears blurred her eyes as those old feelings of failure swept in. Dear heaven, she'd fought hard all her life to throw off the crippling effect of her mother's relentless criticisms by telling herself over and over she was a great person, by developing an extrovert personality, by pretending that nothing and no one could get her down for long. Where was her so-called boldness now when she needed it most?

'Don't,' Kyle said on a raw whisper.

The emotion in his voice startled her into blinking back the tears and staring up at him.

His smile squeezed her heart. 'That's better,' he said. 'The Jade I know doesn't cry over spilt milk. She picks herself up and goes bravely forward, especially when she's got nothing to be ashamed of, except perhaps a little naïveté.' He reached out and laid a tender hand against her cheek. 'Do you trust me, Jade?'

She nodded, his unexpected tenderness bringing a lump to her throat. At least if he was going to reject her, he was going to do it kindly.

'Then I'm going to take you inside, where we're going to have a drink, listen to some music, and then, when the time is right, we'll let nature take its course.'

Her eyes widened, her heart leaping. 'You...you still want to make love to me?'

His laughter was dark and very, very sexy. 'Silly Jade. I've been wanting to make love to you since the moment you opened your father's front door.'

She gasped her surprise.

He chuckled again. 'You've led me a merry dance this past week. One which I hope I'll never have to live through again.'

'But you...you never showed anything,' she said, almost accusingly.

'Perhaps you weren't looking in the right places,' he said drily. 'But enough of such talk. If I'm to be your first successful lover I need all the control I can muster.' He crooked his arm and adopted a po-faced expression. 'Would madam like a grand tour of the houseboat? And perhaps some refreshments after her arduous week?'

Jade giggled before smoothing her face into a parody of his super-cool façade and linking her arm with his. 'I can think of nothing I'd like better.'

The houseboat was one of only a few allowed around Sydney, Kyle told her, adding that he was houseboat-sitting for a Mr Gainsford, who'd gone away on business and wasn't expected back for many months.

'Lucky you,' Jade said with feeling. She couldn't imagine anywhere more delightful to live. In fact, from the moment Jade stepped aboard she was entranced, so much so that any lingering nerves about the night ahead were momentarily distracted by her surroundings. Never had a place taken her eye so much before. And she'd seen plenty of beautiful homes in her privileged life.

It couldn't have been because of the design, which was basic and simple, the A-shaped frame having one huge open-plan room downstairs, surrounded by verandas, and a wooden staircase leading up to a loft which housed the only bedroom.

Maybe it was because everything was made out of wood. The floors, walls, ceilings, fittings, furniture—all were beautifully fashioned and polished, from rich red cedars to light golden pines back to a warm comfortable teak, their shining expanses broken only by thick fluffy cream rugs on the floor, and cool turquoise-coloured cushioning on the sofas and chairs. The downstairs living area contained a huge kitchen and breakfast bar down one end, with a partitioned-off dining section to one side, the rest being devoted to a sitting area and various entertainment equipment.

'Your Mr Gainsford has plenty of money,' she said on seeing the huge range of CDs and videos arranged on shelves beside the CD player. 'And he doesn't like Mozart,' she added teasingly.

'No, he doesn't,' Kyle agreed with a wry smile.

'What does he do?' she asked, curious to know more about this mysterious friend.

Kyle shrugged carelessly. 'He's a businessman. You know the type. Sits on numerous company boards, flits around the world all the time and beds beautiful women left, right and centre. He also has excellent taste in champagne,' he smiled, walking over to open the refrigerator from which he extracted a bottle of the French variety. 'Shall we?'

'Why not?' Jade wandered over to perch up on one of the kitchen stools, having to undo the last button on her jacket to manage it. 'Will he mind, do you think?'

'Not at all. I have permission to use whatever he's left behind.'

'Including the beautiful women?' she asked, thinking of the mystery woman who'd telephoned him.

The bottle popped and Kyle expertly filled two fluted glasses to the brim without any fizzing over. It came to Jade that he'd poured champagne for women he was about to bed many times before, and the thought bothered her. Which was crazy. She didn't mind him being experienced, did she?

When he finished the pouring and looked up, his expression was amused. 'What a loaded question! I refuse

to answer on the grounds it might incriminate me.'
Walking round the breakfast bar, he handed her a glass
before joining her on the closest stool. 'What shall we
drink to?'

'To the generous Mr Gainsford?' she suggested, a
touch tartly.

Kyle laughed. 'Very well. To Mr Gainsford. May he
stay absent.'

They clinked glasses and drank, Jade almost emp-
tying her glass. Champagne was one drink she could
guarantee to make her tipsy in no time flat, especially
on a near-empty stomach, and with the thought of the
inevitable outcome of the evening reviving her earlier
nerves she decided a little intoxication might be on the
agenda. Reaching over, she picked up the bottle and re-
filled her glass, topping up Kyle's as well.

'So tell me, Kyle. How did you get to meet this super-
richy in the first place? Did you work for him at some
stage?'

'No. We—er—went to university together.'

'Really?'

'Most assuredly. He wasn't very popular, I'm afraid.
A terrible snob. And spoiled to boot. Thought his money
could get him anything he wanted.'

Jade wrinkled her nose. 'I don't think I like him very
much.'

'I don't think I did either. Back then. But he's not
such a bad chap nowadays. I'm growing to like him more
and more.'

Jade laughed. 'That's because he's not here. Still, he
must like and trust you to let you stay in his house. Or
is he just using you?'

'Must we keep talking about Gainsford? I'd rather
talk about you. No, quite frankly I'd rather not talk at
all. Bring your glass. I'll bring the bottle. We're going
to bed.'

Jade gasped. 'Just like that?'

'Just like that,' he said, and, picking up the bottle,
slid off the stool.

She slid off her stool as well. 'But you said...'

'I know what I said. I was wrong. I have to make love to you now, Jade. I can't wait any longer.'

The breath hissed from her lungs, her own desire flaring. She stared at his mouth and thought of how it had felt on hers, how it might feel on other parts of her body. Coming forward, he lowered his mouth and kissed her without touching her. It was a soft, lingering erotic kiss that made her shiver uncontrollably.

'You don't really want to wait either,' he said on straightening. 'We don't need hours of foreplay, Jade. This whole week has been foreplay. You and I are as turned on as we're going to get with our clothes on. Any more damned arousing and I won't have a hope in Hades of realising your fantasies about having sex with me.'

'I don't want to *have sex* with you,' she protested. 'I want you to *make love* to me!'

For a moment, he looked taken aback, then he smiled, a highly satisfied smile. 'How silly of me to make such an elementary mistake,' he murmured. 'I'd forgotten the semantics had changed. Make love. Yes, I like that a lot better than having sex. I really do.'

He actually sounded surprised and, brushing past her, walked over towards the wooden staircase in the corner. There he stopped abruptly on the first step, his black eyes glittering and narrowed as he peered back over his shoulder at her. 'Are you in love with me, Jade?'

Her own eyes blinked wide. 'I...I don't know.'

He smiled softly. 'What a lovely honest answer. I do so admire it. And I do so admire you. I won't tell you I love you either, because I too have a problem with that term. Is it enough that I admire you, lovely Jade? Will that do for now?'

Her nod was slow, her head heavy, her thoughts awhirl.

'Are you coming, or are you going to torture me some more?' he said in a drily teasing voice. 'I have a feeling you like seeing men suffer.'

When she stayed standing there, as though frozen, he put down the bottle and the glass and walked back to take the glass from her suddenly trembling hand, draining it with a single swallow. 'You've had enough of this. Let's see if we can't satisfy your other cravings.'

Bending, he swept her up into his arms, smiling ruefully down into her wide-eyed face. 'Who would have thought the outrageous creature who whistled at me last Saturday night was a closet *ingénue*! How intriguing you are, Jade. And how exciting. I'm going to enjoy teaching you to like making love. Not that I think I'll have any trouble. Half the battle is in the wanting to. And you've already confessed to that.'

He carried her as if she were a feather, his strength amazing her. Though tall, he wasn't an overly big man, his muscles lean rather than bulky. But strong he was. Strong and male and totally in command of the situation. Jade was entranced.

'The name suits you,' she whispered on the way upstairs.

'What name?'

'Mr Cool.'

'Mr Cool? Who calls me that?'

'I do.'

'You *do*?' He chuckled his amusement. 'What a minx you are.'

'And a tease.'

'That too. But not for much longer.'

'I'm a little nervous, Kyle.'

'No, you're not. You're excited.'

He set her down on her feet beside the king-sized bed but her knees went from under her and she had to cling to the lapels of his jacket to stop herself from falling back on the bed. Her swaying action reefed the suit jacket wide open.

'What a quick learner you are, darling. I had no idea you'd want to undress me.'

'U-undress you?' she repeated blankly, her heart having leapt wildly with his calling her darling.

'That's the opposite to dress,' he mocked, but not unkindly. 'You know...you undo all the little buttons and zippers and things, instead of doing them up? And when you're finished you haven't got any clothes on. Making

love is much easier when in the nude. Not necessarily
more exciting, mind. The idea of making love to you
with selected clothing on has an exquisitely erotic appeal
but I think we shall leave that for future encounters. For
our first time, I think a certain primitive simplicity is
called for.

'Ah, I see you're getting the picture,' he chuckled when
she pulled the jacket off his shoulders, dragged it down
his arms and tossed it aside to fall she cared not where.
Her heart was going at fifty to the dozen as her fingers
began fumbling with his tie.

'I think you need some help,' he said, and, with one
sharp tug, the tie was loose enough for her to lift it over
his head. It joined the jacket on the floor. The shirt went
in a similar fashion once he'd undone the cuffs and the
top button, over his head and fluttering away.

Now he was naked to the waist and Jade could not
believe how exciting she found that. Quite instinctively,
her hands reached out to touch him, to rove over the
dark curls that covered the centre of his chest and ran
down to where they were terminated abruptly by his
trousers. She could actually feel his heartbeat beneath
her exploring touch, telling her he wasn't nearly as cool
as he pretended.

Jade didn't try to pretend anything. The wanting had
become a need so sharp that she had to resist the urge
to dig her nails into his flesh. As it was, her fingers started
to splay upwards, over his hard male nipples, and up
over his strong, smooth shoulders. Her eyes were glittering blue pools of desire when they looked up, her lips
falling apart in a silent invitation for him to kiss her.

He moved so fast that it was a blur, his mouth crashing
down on hers, his arms crushing her to his naked chest,
a tormented groan rumbling deep in his throat. The realisation that he'd been right about foreplay was echoed
in the rush of heat between her thighs. Jade knew that
this last kiss had brought her to a pitch of need pre-
viously unknown to her. She didn't want to be kissed
any more. She only wanted him.

Tearing her mouth from his, she pressed feverish lips to his throat and whispered her desire in the most explicit terms. The uttering of her need in such a way didn't shock her. It only inflamed her further. She said the words again, biting him this time. She heard his sharply indrawn breath, felt his body flinch, then shudder.

'All right, damn you,' he rasped. 'But don't complain afterwards.'

Any further slow, measured undressing was out of the question. Kyle tore the clothing from her body. Literally tore. Once she was nude, he stopped briefly to stare at her, his breathing ragged. Then suddenly, he pushed her back on to the bed and crushed his body down on hers, spreading her legs, opening her to his desire. Jade had no thought of nerves, or technique or anything, her whole being consumed with nothing but her awareness of his flesh entering hers, filling her totally, making her gasp. His rhythm, when it began, was ruthless and powerful. He went on and on, on and on, till she was clinging to him, writhing with him, moaning with him. She could not believe how it felt. The pleasure, the excitement, the exquisite tension. Till suddenly, it was unbearable.

'Kyle!' she cried out, then groaned in a type of agony. But the agony abruptly shattered into ecstasy and she caught her breath. Her nails dug deep as her body began to spasm, her heart seemingly bursting in her chest. 'Oh, God... Kyle...'

She felt his body begin to shudder, pulsating deep within her, and as she listened to his raw groans of animal pleasure she knew at last what it meant to be primitive woman, what it meant to be sexually satisfied. *And* what it meant to lose her head.

Jade was lying there, still dazed with wonderment at the experience, when she realised they hadn't used anything.

CHAPTER TWELVE

JADE might have bolted up into a sitting position if Kyle hadn't been sprawled across her, his weight pinning her to the bed. But her body must have done something because Kyle lifted his head, opened a sleepy eye and said, 'What?'

'We...we didn't use anything,' she whispered.

He nodded then slumped down again. 'I realised that halfway through.'

Jade was shocked by his casual admission. 'Then why didn't you stop?'

Again his head lifted. This time both eyes were opened and their expression was sardonic. 'You have to be joking. After what you said to me? You're lucky I remembered where the bed was.' He sighed wearily. 'I'm sorry, Jade. Believe me when I tell you that the only misfortune that might befall you is pregnancy. What's the odds of that, do you know?'

'I...I can't think... Oh, God, I don't want to have a baby. I...' Her relief at finally calculating the date of her next period brought a huge sigh. 'I'm due Sunday, thank the lord. For a second, I thought it was the next Sunday. Still, come tomorrow I'm going to the doctor and going on the Pill!'

Kyle rolled from her so abruptly that she gasped. From feeling all warm and cosy she suddenly felt empty and abandoned. He settled himself beside her on his back, staring up at the ceiling. 'Would it have been such a catastrophe, Jade? Having my baby?' His voice was coolly reproachful and it flustered her. As if he would really want her to fall pregnant, anyway.

'Not *your* baby particularly, Kyle,' she explained. '*Any* baby. I'm in my final year at uni and I've just started work at Whitmore's. Do you know how long I've wanted to do that?' She didn't add that she didn't think she'd make a very good mother and hadn't intended to have children.

His head turned on the pillow to stare thoughtfully over at her. 'What do you want out of life, Jade? Besides my job.'

Her laughter was slightly embarrassed. 'So you know about that, do you?'

'Of course. I told you. Your face is an open book.'

'I'm quite happy to let you have the job a while longer,' she said teasingly. 'Till I've learnt all I can from you.'

He slanted her a mocking look. 'Are we still talking about work here?'

Realisation what he was inferring brought a fierce blush to her cheeks. 'Surely you don't think that I...that I...'

His smile was reassuring as he rolled on to his side. 'I do love it when you're flustered like that. It's so sweet.'

'I'm not sweet. I'm spicy, remember?'

'Mmm.' His fingers started feathering over her breasts and she caught her breath, still amazed at how his touch made her feel. 'You have a beautiful body,' he murmured. 'Your mother must have been a beautiful woman.'

Jade flinched inside. 'Yes,' she said stiffly. 'She was. *Physically.*'

His fingers stilled, his eyes thoughtful upon her. 'What do you mean by that?'

She shrugged, trying desperately to ignore the pain jabbing at her heart.

'Didn't you get along with your mother, Jade? Look, I know she died recently. Byron told me. If you're feeling guilty about something then perhaps you should talk about it.'

'*Me*, feel guilty?' she scorned bitterly. 'That would be a laugh. I've nothing to feel guilty about. My only regret is that death allowed my mother to escape before I had the courage to tell her what I thought of her, to tell her what an evil, wicked witch she was!'

Her tirade finished, Jade lay trembling in the bed, till Kyle gathered her close, his strong warm body soothing her, as his words soothed her. 'You're wrong, Jade. Her death was a blessed release. For everyone around her. She must have been a terrible person and a terrible mother to make you feel about her like this.'

'I think she hated me, Kyle,' she cried. 'And I keep asking myself why. She used to hit me a lot when I was little. Not when my father was around, of course. If Nathan hadn't come to live with us...' Jade broke off, a lump filling her throat.

'Nathan stopped her?' Kyle asked gently.

'I don't know,' she choked out. 'Maybe. Or maybe his just being there stopped her. Auntie Ava was away at school at the time. After that, it was just verbal abuse. I couldn't do a thing right. She even made Pops believe I was bad. Bad and worthless. Why would she want to do that? Mothers arc supposed to *love* their children.'

'I don't know, Jade. She must have been sick in the head, or just plain mean. There are people like that. Mean and sour and cruel. But she didn't succeed in turning your father against you, darling. Your father thinks the sun shines out of you. He does worry about you—you are a little wild, darling, and totally outrageous at times—but all in all, he's coming around to my way of thinking.'

'Your way of thinking?'

'That his daughter is an exceptional girl. Talented and bright, if a tad provocative. You might benefit from wearing a bra occasionally. Though I won't complain at the moment.' He laid her back on the pillow and slid an outstretched palm back and forth across the tips of her breasts, making her lungs expand with an inward rush of breath. Soon, her mother was forgotten and she was breathless with desire and need again. She started touching him back, more boldly than she'd ever touched a man before.

'I've never wanted a man the way I want you,' she whispered, all the while caressing him. 'Why is that, do you think?'

'Maybe you've fallen in love for the first time,' he suggested thickly.

'Would it worry you if I told you I loved you? A lot of men would run a mile.'

'*Do* you love me?'

'I'm still not sure. I've thought myself in love in the past and now I can see I never was. Not once. Have you ever been in love, Kyle?'

'Never.'

Was that a pain deep in her breast when he said that? Could that be a sign of true love, when it hurt if the man you were touching so intimately said he didn't love you? No, no, she'd been hurt when Nathan rejected her. That couldn't be an infallible sign.

'Whatever I feel,' she whispered, 'I know I loved it when you made love to me. I love the feel of your body. I love everything about you...'

He grabbed her hands and held them up over her head, looming over her with dark glittering eyes.

'And I love everything about you, my darling Jade. Every...single...thing...'

He kissed her, very slowly, as though he were savouring something delicious but didn't want to rush. First just her bottom lip, then her upper, then both. When his tongue finally slipped into her mouth, her breath caught. She'd never been kissed so lasciviously before. His tongue swept sensuously around the soft well of her mouth, before slowly withdrawing. Her own tongue followed as though magnetised. Now it was deep in *his* mouth and her excitement soared. He groaned, his hands cupping her head while he regained control of the kiss. By the time he stopped, her whole mouth felt all swollen and tingling.

'Might as well be hung for a sheep as a lamb,' he muttered, and he rolled them both on to their sides, hoisting her left knee high on his hip, his flesh slipping inside her very easily. Jade sighed her pleasure as his hips moved gently back and forth, creating the most delicious feelings. His fingers started feathering over her nipples at the same time and she moaned softly.

'Would you like to be on top?' he asked in a desire-thickened voice.

'I... I don't know,' she said breathlessly. 'I've never been there.'

His smile was rueful. 'Don't get too used to it.'

'Thank God it's Friday!' Jade exclaimed to Moira as she hurried in to work shortly before two, letting the glass doors swing shut behind her. The doors weren't the only things that were swinging. The skirt of Jade's white woollen suit was finely pleated and quite short.

'Amen to that,' Moira sighed. 'This last week has been very trying.'

'You can say that again,' someone muttered from just behind Jade.

She whirled round to find Kyle striding towards her. He must have come from the direction of the design rooms. Or the gents'. He looked tense and almost angry, strain giving his leanly chiselled features the sort of primitive, brooding look she found insidiously attractive. The black suit and crisp white shirt he had on didn't detract from his appeal either, making his black eyes seem even darker and more intense.

Jade stared at him as though he were a chocolate éclair and she were a compulsive eater. It had been a whole week since he'd touched her, and she was on fire for him. Working with him all Wednesday had been an ordeal, sleeping at night since then a problem. She hadn't realised her frustration was so intense till she sighted him again in the flesh.

Kyle glared at her, his facial muscles tightening. Taking her elbow, he ushered her towards their office. 'You're just in time, Jade,' he ground out. 'I've had nothing but hassles all day and now another problem has come up.'

'Not the date with the ball!' she groaned. 'That PR woman at the Regency doesn't want to change it again, does she?'

'No, that's not it,' he ground out once they were alone and the door shut. Reefing her bag from her arm, he threw it in the corner, took her by the shoulders and yanked her against him, kissing her savagely. A shocked

Jade did nothing when he urged her back against the solid wooden door, but she soon realised that if his marauding tongue was anything to go by she was dealing with an even more frustrated individual than she was.

'You're late,' he growled after the most arousing minute she'd ever endured.

'You're the one who wouldn't let me bring my car,' she reminded him breathlessly, before curving her hand around his neck and dragging his mouth back to hers for another dose of erotic torment.

This is crazy, she was thinking all the while. We can't do anything here. Why torture ourselves?

Jade was underestimating her Mr Cool, however, who was far from cool at this moment.

'I like you in white,' he rasped into her mouth while busy fingers flicked open the buttons of her jacket. 'But I like you better in nothing.' Jade stiffened against the door when he started kneading her bare breasts. When he bent to draw a rock-like nipple into his white-hot mouth everything inside her contracted fiercely, desire bursting like a firecracker in her head.

'Kyle, don't,' she groaned. God, if he kept that up she was going to go mad! Her sigh of relief when he deserted her breasts was short-lived. Kyle was merely homing in on a more intimate destination.

The scrap of white silk and lace she was wearing was highly inadequate protection against an impassioned man. He simply tore it aside. Jade bit her bottom lip some more, though a small cry did escape her lips when Kyle achieved what he was bent on achieving. But dear heaven, he felt fantastic. A flush of heat zoomed into her cheeks and she just had to lick her lips, they were so dry.

'What...what if someone wants to come in?' she asked, her voice shaking.

'Can't think about that right now.'

'N...neither can I. Oh, Kyle...'

No one wanted to come in. Thank God.

Afterwards, Jade couldn't believe what they had just done. But she had plenty to remind her. Half-wrecked panties for one.

'You...you do realise we're supposed to take added precautions for the first month I'm on this Pill,' she reminded him shakily after she slumped down in her chair behind the desk.

'Yes,' he said, striding round to sit at his own desk, looking so cool and unruffled now that Jade felt a fierce flash of resentment.

'Well? You didn't just now. *Again.*'

His glance was wry. 'You do seem to have a bad effect on my normal precautionary nature.'

She wasn't at all mollified by his amused tone. In fact, she was rather rattled by the whole encounter. 'I...I hope this isn't all our relationship is going to be, Kyle. Sex in the office on Fridays.'

'I certainly hope not. I'll add Wednesdays to the agenda in future. And when did it become sex instead of making love?' he asked with an arched eyebrow.

'You can ask that with me sitting here at my desk with wrecked panties?'

God, but he was sexy when he smiled like that. But so damned arrogant, so damned sure of himself.

'I don't want our relationship reduced to just sex,' she argued.

'I couldn't agree more,' he countered drily. 'I already asked you to move in with me last weekend, if you recall. But you said no. You also wouldn't go out with me this past week, simply because you had a period. That's rather reducing our relationship to just sex, wouldn't you say? I wouldn't have minded simply spending time with you.'

Jade winced under the interpretation he'd put on her actions. But it hadn't been like that at all. When she'd woken last Saturday morning to find Kyle bringing her breakfast and calmly suggesting she move in with him, she'd been consumed with panic, and an intense desire just to get away from him. Perhaps it was her natural tendency to resist others organising her life which gave rise to her sudden desperate need for personal space. Or perhaps she'd been frightened by how much she kept wanting him, how tempted she'd been to just say yes to everything and anything.

Which was why she was uncomfortable with what had just happened in the office. She hadn't meant to let him go so far but she'd simply lost control. She didn't like losing control like that! And yet...it had been incredibly exciting. Was this what happened when lust got its claws into you? Did it make you vulnerable to the point of losing your own identity? Bewilderment brought irritation. And a rise of temper.

'It wasn't just my period,' she reiterated crossly. 'I had to finish an assignment.'

'You could have finished it at my place.'

She laughed. 'Oh, yes? I don't think so, Kyle. You're far too distracting.'

'If you lived with me all the time, we'd soon settle into a less distracting mode. And then I wouldn't have to rip your clothes off against office doors. I certainly can't cope with working in the same room as you, my darling Jade, if you're going to put me on rations.' His smile was wickedly seductive. 'Come now...you usually live away from home, don't you? Byron said you did.'

'Not with a man, I don't,' she said, all the while horribly tempted. 'I think single women are crazy to live with men they're not married to.'

'So *that's* the problem. All right. Name the date.'

'Oh, don't be ridiculous, Kyle. You don't love me. Why would you marry me? Besides, I have no intention of ever getting married, or having babies for that matter! Now I really must go to the ladies'.'

Jade dashed for the door before she threw herself at him and just said yes to whatever he wanted of her. But while she hurried along the corridor, she kept thinking about the look she'd glimpsed on Kyle's face. He'd seemed quite put out. Surely he hadn't meant that off-the-cuff proposal, had he? No, he couldn't have, she dismissed, though not without a sharp contraction of her heart. He didn't love her. It was 'making love' to her he loved. He'd made that pretty clear on Friday night. Not to mention just now.

She was drying her hands after a visit to the loo when a sickening thought struck. Maybe he *had* meant it. But not for reasons of love...

She was the boss's daughter, wasn't she? A lot of ambitious men married the boss's daughter to get ahead. Her own father had married her mother with one eye on the Campbell fortune.

Another, even more appalling thought invaded her stunned brain. Twice, Kyle had not taken precautions when having sex with her. Twice, he'd risked her getting pregnant. Yet he was a very clever, cool individual who wouldn't make silly mistakes or take silly risks.

Her heart squeezed even tighter. God, could he do something as wicked as that—seduce her, make her pregnant, then marry her simply to further his ambition? She recalled Kyle looking assessingly around Belleview, and the way he'd ingratiated himself with her father.

I'm being paranoid again, she finally decided. Kyle's not like that. I just know he's not!

But she was not entirely convinced as she slowly made her way back to the office, her mind racing over everything she knew about him, which was...not very much. She didn't even know anything about his family.

A grim-faced Kyle was on the telephone when she re-entered the room.

'I see,' he was saying as she sat down at her desk. 'So that's how she manages it. Clever bitch. But unless we give the tour companies and guides kickbacks as well, our stores will keep on being bypassed in favour of Campbell's. And Byron won't do that... What's that? No, I can't see how we can take legal action, but I might leak the story to a few of the television stations. Campbell Jewels won't smell too good by the time I'm finished, and neither will Celeste Campbell... Yes, well, you're welcome to her. She's not my type, I can tell you. I like warm, loving women, not bloodsucking vampires... Yes, thanks, Peter. You've done wonders.'

He hung up, his expression pensive as he leant back and fiddled with a Biro. Jade couldn't tell if he was deliberately ignoring her, or was genuinely preoccupied. She decided the only way to handle her nervous curiosity about him was to be upfront and honest. He said he liked that about her.

'Kyle,' she began somewhat hesitantly.

His black gaze drifted her way, finally focusing on her. 'Yes?'

'Do you have any brothers or sisters?'

He snapped forward in his chair. 'No. I'm an only child.'

'And are your parents still living?'

'What is this? Twenty questions?'

'No. I...I realised while I was in the ladies' that I didn't know much about you. On a personal basis, that is.'

'What's prompted this sudden need for more details?'

'You won't get mad if I tell you the truth?'

'I'll try not to.'

'I...I began wondering if you could have been serious about asking me to marry you, even though you don't love me. I even started worrying you were *trying* to get me pregnant...'

'Now why would I do a silly thing like that?' he returned coolly.

'To marry the boss's daughter?' she suggested, trying to keep her voice teasingly light.

His smile sent an odd shiver rippling down her spine. 'If that was my intention then why would I have stopped off at the chemist to buy protection the other night on the way home?'

'You did? Well...well...you didn't use it, did you? Just tell me straight, Kyle,' she persisted bravely. '*Is* that your intention?'

'What?'

'To make me marry you?'

'Good God, no.'

'You don't have to sound so appalled! I'm not that bad, am I?'

'No, of course not, but any wife of mine will come to me willingly. Which reminds me, I take it you'll be coming home with me tonight?'

'Maybe. Maybe not.'

He laughed. 'That won't work a second time, Jade. Now come over here. I have a mind to...'

A tap on the office door was followed by a barked 'come' from Kyle and Moira popping her head inside.

'Byron wants to see Jade for a tick.'

'I...I wonder what he wants?' Jade asked, her head still whirling from what Kyle had had a mind to do. God, but she was like putty in his hands. All that garbage she'd told herself about not wanting him to make love to her in the office had been just that: garbage. It was clear he could have her any time he wanted. And the thought excited her unbearably.

In a way, she was happy to flee his seductive presence, even if meetings with her father were also fraught with danger. Nathan's prognostication that he might have mellowed had been way off track. He was as difficult and demanding as ever.

'Ah, there you are,' he gruffed on her entering his office and closing the door. 'I just wanted to ask if you needed a lift home tonight.'

'Oh—er—no. I think I'll go out after work.'

'All night again, I suppose,' he bit out. 'Like last Friday night.'

Jade declined to answer. She was not a child and refused to be treated like one. Her father heaved a ragged sigh.

'Well, sit down while you're here and tell me how you and Kyle are getting along. He speaks warmly of you, says you have a sharp business brain and a flair for marketing.'

'That's generous of him.'

'Kyle's not generous. He's got one of the toughest and best business brains I've ever encountered. You must be doing something right to impress him as much as you do.'

Heat zoomed into her cheeks. Say something, for pity's sake, she told herself swiftly, before he guesses the truth!

'By the way, Pops, did Kyle mention our plans for the ball? And did he ask you about the Heart of Fire?'

'Yes, he did. A ball like that will cost a lot of money, you know. Still, I promised to give Kyle his head for a while. As for the Heart of Fire, do whatever you want with the damned thing. Frankly, I'll be glad to see the back of it. That opal's brought Whitmore's nothing but bad luck and heartache. Far better it finds another owner. Of course, I would like to see it bought by a collector, not someone who's going to have it cut up. Gemma would have my hide if we allowed that to happen.'

Jade smiled to herself. Fancy her tough businessman of a father caring what Gemma felt about an opal she didn't even own. The girl had a way with her, there was no doubt about that.

'It would bring far more if sold as a collector's piece, anyway,' Jade said. 'We'll advertise it as such and display it in the window of the Regency Hotel store. A lot of wealthy people pass that way and I'm sure its auction at the ball will draw a lot of avid collectors. And if it brings what it's worth, believe me it'll bring *good* luck to Whitmore's, not bad. A million dollars will finance some of the changes we're going to adopt. Nothing like some cash flow to soothe the bank manager's hesitancy to give us any loans we want.'

Byron stared at her. 'You sound as if you know what you're talking about, daughter.'

'I do, Pops, I do. Now when can I have a look at this treasure?'

'No time like the present. I'll get it for you and you can show Kyle.'

It was magnificent, there was no doubt about that. And huge! Though unless one turned it over to the side where the rough stone had been sliced away to reveal the opal inside, it looked like a useless piece of gray potch.

'What happened back in the olden days with this opal, Pops?' she asked as she turned it this way and that, dazzled by the pinfire flashes of changing colour. 'Did Grandfather find it and refuse to share it with Mr. Campbell? Is that what started the original feud?'

'I have no idea,' her father said, so curtly that Jade knew for certain he *did* know the truth. It had to be something really awful, she decided, something that made David Whitmore look very bad. She also knew there was no point in keeping on asking her father about it, because his handsomeness was only exceeded by his stubbornness.

Byron Whitmore's main failing in life, his daughter believed, was his maniacal clinging to the family's good reputation, at all cost. That was why he hadn't divorced his wife, why Jade herself had been such a trial to him as a teenager. Nothing was to sully the good name of the Whitmores. Which was why Jade had been so upset—and shocked—when she'd caught him kissing their last housekeeper.

Not that she cared about that so much now. She wasn't so shocked any more, either. Heavens, if she couldn't appreciate how her father could turn to another woman after being married to her mother for all those years ...

'Pops,' she said abruptly. 'Why was Mum the way she was?'

Byron shook his head, sighing. 'She was a very unhappy woman, Jade. Very ... disturbed.'

'Yes, but *why*? Tell me the truth. It's important to me and I'm old enough, surely.'

His taut face told her he didn't agree. 'I don't like to talk ill of the dead.'

'Pops, I think she *hated* me. I want to know why.'

'No, Jade, it wasn't *you* she hated.'

'Well, it wasn't *you*. She was crazy about you.'

Jade used to be amazed at the change in her mother when Byron came home. If ever there was a Jekyll and Hyde character, it was Irene Campbell Whitmore.

'She loved me and she hated me,' Byron said grimly.

'But why? Was it because she found out you didn't love her?'

His face paled with shock. 'How did you know about...?'

'Everyone knows, Pops,' she cut in drily.

'*Everyone*?'

'Well, everyone in the family.'

'What...what do they know?'

'That you married Mum because you thought she was going to inherit Campbell Jewels.'

He stared at her hard, then dropped his eyes and shook his head. 'I had no idea...'

'It's all right, Pops. I forgive you. It's all water under the bridge now. I just needed some answers.'

His eyes lifted, eyes as blue as the sea and just as unfathomable. 'Well, now you have them. Believe me, if I did wrong, daughter, I suffered for it.'

And so did I, Jade thought ruefully. But at least it wasn't my fault. It wasn't that I was unlovable but that my mother was not right in the head. Jade felt as if a huge weight had been lifted from her soul.

She stood up, the opal in her hands, keen now to take it back to show Kyle.

'Is that to hit me with?' the younger man mocked on seeing the opal, which did look like a chunk of stone.

'Do you deserve hitting?' she teased, walking over to slide up on to the corner of his desk, crossing her legs and placing the opal before him. 'There it is. The Heart of Fire. What do you think of it?'

He dragged in then exhaled a ragged breath. 'I think...that if you don't want to have sex in the office...then I suggest you get off my desk immediately.'

His eyes were fixed on her thighs and Jade felt the thrill of real sexual power. It compelled her to push things further. She began swinging her leg in a slow, tantalising fashion, and watched in fascination as his fists curled over, his knuckles going white.

'I just might have changed my mind about that,' she husked. 'I've decided I like having my own toy-boy on tap.'

'Get off this desk, Jade,' he bit out. 'Now!'

Startled by his angry outburst, she slipped off the desk, laughing nervously. 'Sorry. I ... I didn't realise you were so lacking in control.'

Jade scuttled back towards her desk, a glance back over her shoulder stopping her in her tracks. Never had she seen Kyle look like that. Was he shocked, or in pain?

'What?' she gasped. 'What is it?'

His expression slowly hardened to one of cold fury. 'I can see I've damaged my Mr Cool image in your eyes, Jade,' he said with icy disdain. 'I doubt you even respect me as a man any more. How perverse ... Still, the situation is not irretrievable. We will simply have to abandon our affair and return to our previous *status quo*. Yes, I really do think that would be best. This isn't going to work.'

Initially, Jade froze with shock. But once she accepted that Kyle meant every word he said, her legs went to water. She had to lean on the desk for support. 'You ... you don't mean that, Kyle.'

His expression was so aloof, she shivered.

'I'm afraid you don't know me very well, Jade. Except in the biblical sense,' he added with a sardonic twist to his mouth. 'But I can assure you that, as of now, any physical intimacy between us has ceased. We will revert to boss and assistant, unless, of course, you only came to work with me for sexual gratification,' he finished derisively. 'In which case you can quit right now.'

'You know that's not true!'

'Do I?'

Jade's hands lifted to her temples which had begun to pound. 'Why ... why are you doing this?' she cried. 'A little while ago you wanted me to move in with you. What's changed? What have I said or done?'

'I don't have to explain myself to you, Jade. Neither do I have to keep risking my position here simply to get my rocks off.'

Jade felt the nausea rising in her stomach. 'Is that what you were doing earlier? Getting your rocks off?'

'What else?'

She stared at him, horror and hurt in her eyes.

'I have to go out now, Jade. I suggest you get on with your promotional work regarding the ball. Oh, and you'd better ask your father for a lift home. You're going to be needing it.'

Jade managed to hold herself together till he left, then she collapsed, sobbing, at her desk.

people even thinking she had problems. He'd never

CHAPTER THIRTEEN

'I'M GOING to miss you,' Kirsty wailed, and threw her arms around Gemma.

'Me too,' Gemma whispered, tears pricking her eyes. This would probably be the last time that Kirsty would look at her with such affection. By this time next week, she would be Nathan's wife and Kirsty's new step-mother. God knew what the shock was going to do to their friendship. Gemma didn't like to think about it.

'We're only down the road, for heaven's sake!' Lenore complained. 'Gemma can visit whenever she likes, and so can you, Kirsty. Anyone would think you were going overseas, not a suburb away!'

Both girls looked at each other and laughed. They were in Kirsty's bedroom, which had been transformed back to its previous pink and white prettiness, the rock posters and geometric quilt now installed in her bedroom at home, much to Lenore's disgust.

Jade wandered in, looking far from her usual perky self. 'We're going to miss you, darls,' she told Kirsty, and gave her a hug.

'Come along now, Kirsty,' Lenore pleaded. 'I have a performance tonight. We have to go.'

It was Easter Thursday, the last day of the school term, and the last day in March. Kirsty's school had only had a half-day of classes and Lenore was using the free afternoon to get her daughter moved home.

They all trailed downstairs, and after a flurry of further goodbyes they were gone. Gemma watched Jade turn to walk slowly upstairs, head down, shoulders slumped.

There was definitely something wrong with her. But Jade was a hard person to talk to about personal matters. Her bright, extrovert personality formed a barrier against people even *thinking* she had problems, let alone asking her about them. Gemma had tried the other night, and what had Jade done? Brushed her query aside with a laugh and an excuse.

'I'm just tired, darls,' she'd said. 'This working business is a lot tougher than I thought it would be. I think I'd better have an early night.' With that, she'd gone to her room.

In her own way, Jade could be as difficult to pin down and discuss something with as Nathan could be.

Gemma's frown deepened as her mind shifted to the man who would become her husband within seven days. She loved Nathan deeply—in fact was crazy about him—but they still hadn't discussed basic issues such as children, not to mention where they would even live. Nathan's announcement that he would be moving permanently to Avoca after Easter had startled her till she realised he'd said that to ensure Kirsty went home to live. He couldn't really mean to live there, not when she was supposed to start work at the Regency Hotel store, four days after their planned wedding on the Thursday afternoon.

But she hadn't been able to discuss anything private and personal with Nathan since that interlude in her bedroom three weeks before, simply because they hadn't been alone together since, except for a couple of times briefly in the hallway, and on the stairs. On each occasion, someone had come along to interrupt their conversation and they hadn't been able to talk at length. Tonight, however, she was determined to find out what Nathan's plans were, even if she had to go to his bedroom.

This thought immediately unnerved her, not because she thought Nathan would try to make love to her, but because she knew he wouldn't. The waiting leading up to her wedding night had been as nerve-racking as she'd envisaged. She wasn't sleeping well and when she did her dreams were disturbingly erotic. On one occasion, they'd been quite frightening.

She'd dreamt she was naked and tied to a chair in Nathan's den at the beach-house. She'd been freezing cold and was begging Nathan to untie her. But he'd sat at his computer, writing and ignoring her pleas. Finally, he'd looked up at her and coldly told her that he didn't like little girls who begged, that she was to shut up and not say a word till he decided he wanted her again.

She'd awoken from the dream, sobbing. It had been the last she had slept that night.

Thinking about that dream now sent a *frisson* of fear rippling down her spine, and she quickly decided against going to Nathan's room tonight, or asking him anything. She knew it was weak of her, and silly. She had every right to know these things. But somehow, that dream had undermined her faith in Nathan's love for her, as well as her faith in her own judgement.

Suddenly, she bolted upstairs and ran into her room, shutting the door and turning the lock.

'He wouldn't hurt me,' she whispered out loud to herself. 'Not my Nathan.'

But she started to shiver uncontrollably, and, no matter what she did, an inner chill remained. Finally, she sat down and wrote a long letter to Ma. It was a light, newsy letter which not once mentioned Nathan or her coming marriage. It was as though if she wrote it down it might not come about. Or was she afraid that Ma would advise her against the marriage, would make her face things she didn't want to face, things buried so deep in her subconscious that they only surfaced in her dreams?

'*Married*!' Ava squawked, her plump face going pink.

'Married?' Jade repeated, as though she'd never heard of the institution.

'Married,' Byron said slowly, nodding with quiet satisfaction at his adopted son.

Melanie, who'd been standing at the dining-table, serving the entrée, when Nathan and Gemma walked in, simply stared at them both.

'Yes, married,' Nathan said, and tightened his grip around Gemma's shoulder. 'We didn't say anything before because we didn't want any fuss. And we don't want any now,' he added, his tone and eyes whipping round the gathering at the dining-table. 'In fact, we're about to leave on an extended honeymoon, first at the Regency over the weekend and then at Avoca. I'm afraid Gemma won't be starting work next week after all, Byron. That will have to be delayed for a while.'

'Of course, Nathan, of course. A new bride won't be wanting to work.' He stood up and came forward, all magnanimous smiles.

The three women did not move, their eyes no longer shocked, Gemma thought, but pitying. Strangely, she didn't find their pity annoying, but disturbing. They're afraid for me, she realised, and trembled.

Nathan's head jerked down, his expression concerned. She looked up into his eyes and was sure she saw real love there. Or was she just hoping?

Suddenly, Byron was upon them and Nathan had to let her go to accept his adopted father's congratulatory hug.

'I can't tell you how pleased I am, Nathan. You've chosen well this time. And Gemma, my love...' He turned to her and took both her hands, bending to kiss her on the cheek. 'I couldn't ask for a lovelier daughter-in-law. I know you'll make Nathan happy, my dear.'

'We must away, Byron. I have a limousine waiting.'

'A limousine, no less,' he chuckled warmly. 'I'm impressed. You've finally learnt the way to a woman's heart, have you?'

'I think so,' Nathan said with an odd little smile.

Gemma shivered again, and Nathan slid an arm around her waist, giving her a little squeeze. 'Say goodbye to everyone, darling.'

She said goodbye to everyone, and was about to let Nathan guide her firmly from the room when she broke free from his hold and dashed back to kiss each woman in turn, thanking them profusely for everything and saying a whispered 'forgive me' in each ear. Tears in her eyes, she fled back to her husband's arms and was quickly spirited away.

The limousine swallowed her up, the heavily tinted windows giving her an even more claustrophobic feeling which she found smothering and depressing. A great feeling of sadness suddenly overwhelmed her. Tears were streaming down her face by the time Nathan climbed in beside her and the car moved off. He took one look and gathered her against his chest, stroking her hair, while she cried and cried.

'Let it all out,' he soothed. 'You'll be better soon. Much better. It's the tension, you see ...'

He talked to her gently and kindly, his embrace sweet and tender. Gemma hardly noticed the moment when the privacy partition slid upwards and the seduction began. It was all done so slowly, so smoothly, and so expertly that she didn't stand a chance from the start. And when it was over, and she lay replete and totally relaxed in her husband's arms, she could hardly remember those few moments of panic when she'd realised what Nathan was going to do. Or those other earlier fears. That all seemed irrelevant now, and far, far away.

'Happy, Mrs Whitmore?' came the husky query, moist lips pressed against her throat.

'Mmm,' she sighed.

'We'd better get you dressed, then. We'll be arriving at the hotel soon.'

Jade lay on her bed, staring up at the ceiling.

Married.

Nathan and Gemma were married.

She couldn't believe it. He'd actually *married* her. Suddenly, she sat up.

Lenore! Did she know? And what about Kirsty? Oh, the poor kid. She had set her heart on her parents eventually getting back together again. Of course, everyone else had known that would never happen, but they'd also all thought Nathan would never marry again either. Kirsty having to face the reality of her father having a new bride would be shattering to her. Having that bride be Gemma would only make things worse. Gemma had been Kirsty's friend, more than her minder.

Jade jumped up and ran downstairs to find her father. He was in the library, reading.

'Pops,' she said abruptly, startling him. 'Does Lenore know?'

He frowned. 'I don't know.'

'I think someone should tell her, don't you?'

'Surely Nathan would have told her.'

'What if he hasn't?'

'Mmm. I need to speak to Lenore anyway. Look, I'll call her straight away and find out, then I'll come and tell you what the situation is.'

'OK. I'll be in the kitchen, having some hot chocolate.'

Byron heaved a troubled sigh as his daughter left the room.

Damn! What if Nathan *hadn't* told Lenore and Kirsty? It would be darned irresponsible if he hadn't. And inconsiderate. There again, Nathan could be like that sometimes.

Byron brooded for a moment, remembering the mess Nathan had been in when he'd found him all those years ago up at King's Cross. There were times when Byron wondered if he'd done the right thing, adopting Nathan, bringing him into his own home. But he'd been compelled to try to rescue the boy from the corruption and depravity surrounding him. How could he leave him there in the clutches of that evil woman? She had been screwing up his mind, as well as his body. Byron shuddered to think what she'd already made the boy believe about the male sex.

Byron had been proud of what he'd made of the lad. Why, he'd turned him round from a potential lost soul to a man of good character and moral strength. A decent man. Admittedly, he did worry sometimes about Nathan's tendency to withdraw emotionally from those around him, yet one only had to read his plays to know that he had more emotions within him than a hundred men. But perhaps writing was the only way he could express it. Maybe when it came right down to his relationships with people—especially women—he could only operate on the level he'd been taught, first by example, and then by experience.

No, Byron thought with sudden venom. I refuse to believe that. He's changed since those days. Grown. Matured. And Gemma's right for him. I knew that from the start. Her very innocence will be his salvation. He wouldn't dare try to corrupt that. Or take advantage of it. At least . . . I hope not.

'Damn! Damn! Damn!'

Byron levered himself to his feet, cursing more colourfully when a sharp pain shot through his thigh. Would this bastard of a leg never get better? Limping slightly, he made his way over to the desk and the address book he kept next to the phone. Flicking over the pages, he looked up Lenore's number and dialled. She'd probably be home, he knew, because the play she'd been in had folded at the weekend after a very short run. Comedies never did as well as dramas, in his opinion.

Lenore answered on the second ring.

'Byron here, Lenore. I have some news for you which you may or may not already know.'

'If you're referring to Nathan's marriage to Gemma,' she said with a disgruntled sigh, 'I already know. Nathan rang me earlier.'

'Have you told Kirsty?'

'Yes.'

'How's she taking it?'

'Badly.'

'Is there anything I can do? Or Jade? We were worried.'

'Not really, Byron. At least Kirsty's now coming to terms with our divorce being permanent, but she's cut up about Gemma. I've tried explaining that she should blame her father, not that unfortunate child, but I guess she feels betrayed.'

'Why do you say unfortunate child?' Byron snapped.

'Oh, for God's sake, Byron, don't you have any idea what Nathan's like? He doesn't see a female as anything other than a sexual partner, to be manipulated and programmed to his needs.'

'That's not true this time, Lenore. He loves the girl!'

'If he does then I only pity her the more. He'll leave no stone unturned till he's made her his to the exclusion of everything else. I was lucky because I *didn't* love him. Despite that, he didn't do a bad job of enslaving my senses, since I stayed married to him for so long. But in the end, Byron, sex alone just wasn't enough. I needed love. Real love. Gemma will too.'

'Nathan really loves Gemma, Lenore. I'm sure of it.'

'But does she really love him? Or is she just infatuated by Nathan's glamour and sexual sophistication? If so, then you'll have another divorce on your hands once she starts growing up.'

'She's grown up already,' he pronounced stubbornly, unwilling to accept the sense of what Lenore was saying.

'Oh, Byron, don't be ridiculous. She's just a child.'

'I don't like you talking like this!'

'You don't like anyone telling you how it is, Byron. You never have.'

'Humph! And you've always had an acid tongue, Lenore. You won't find yourself another man if you don't learn to curb it.'

'Oh, really?'

Byron heard the smugness in her voice, and frowned. 'So that's how the land lies, eh? Who's fallen into your clutches this time?'

'That's my business.'

Lenore's uneasy tone of voice sent a ghastly suspicion popping into his head. 'Who is he, Lenore? I want to know.'

'As I said, it's none of your business.'

'Maybe. Maybe not. If you don't tell me, our other deal is off.'

'But you promised!'

'A verbal contract with no witnesses is no contract at all.'

Lenore muttered something very uncomplimentary. 'All right, though why you want to know I've no idea. It's Zachary Marsden. There! I hope you're happy.'

'*Zachary*?' Byron was astonished. He'd been worried that maybe Lenore had become mixed up with Damian Campbell. He'd seen that snake hanging around her at parties a few times, oozing his brand of charm. The younger of the two Campbell heirs, he was sinfully handsome and had turned plenty of women's heads, most of them married. He was a lecher of the first order.

Still, lechery ran in the family.

Byron stiffened and dragged his mind back out of the cesspool that started swirling in his mind. God, would he never get that damned woman out of his mind?

'Might I remind you, Lenore,' Byron lectured, 'that Zachary is a happily married man?'

Lenore sighed her frustration. 'I hate to disillusion you about *two* members of your sex tonight, Byron. But Zachary is far from happily married. In fact, Felicity recently asked him for a divorce and when it comes through next year wc will be getting married. Till then we're keeping our relationship a secret. I'm only telling you this because you've forced it out of me, but if you mention it to a soul, I swear, Byron, I will come round and impale you with that walking stick of yours!'

Byron only just managed not to chuckle. He had to give Lenore credit for courage and spirit. As for Zachary... maybe he even envied him a little. Lenore was a beauty all right, and a very passionate woman, if he was any judge. She reminded him a little of...

Byron clamped his teeth down hard in his jaw.

'I won't tell anyone, Lenore,' he bit out. 'And you'll have the lead role in Nathan's new play, as promised. Nathan doesn't want any say in the production, I asked him. I'll contact you next week once I've lined up a director and a theatre.'

Byron hung up before she could say another word, taking a while before he remembered the original purpose of the call. Rising, he went in search of Jade. At least Nathan had done the right thing and told Lenore himself, but after what Lenore had said he had to admit he was worried about Nathan's marriage to Gemma now, which was a shame. He'd been so happy about it before, had really felt they were made for one another. Who knew? Maybe *his* gut feelings would be proved right in the end, and not Lenore's. She had to be biased, after all. Nathan had not loved her. But he did love Gemma. Byron was sure of it.

'How's Kirsty bearing up?' Jade asked Lenore as they wandered together through the shopping arcade. A week had passed since Nathan's and Gemma's marriage, a week during which hardly a word had been spoken at Belleview about the hopefully happy couple. Everyone seemed to be reluctant to give voice to an opinion, adopting a more wait and see attitude. 'Pops told me she was upset,' Jade added.

'She's a little better. A letter arrived from Gemma which made her cry again, but with more understanding this time, though no real forgiveness. I read the letter myself and to be honest I cried too. That poor girl sounded terribly upset to think we might not like her any more because of her marrying Nathan. She's so sweet, Jade, but so naïve. Nathan deserves to be shot for marrying her.'

'I don't agree. I'm rather proud of him.'

Lenore's green eyes snapped round. '*Proud*?'

'Yes. He didn't have to marry her to have her, Lenore. We both know that. He could have simply used her, as so many men do young girls, then tossed her aside. Even if the marriage doesn't last, this way her rights are protected by law. Gemma will at least be financially secure for life.'

'Financially secure and emotionally destroyed,' Lenore said acidly.

'We'll see...'

'What exactly are we shopping for tonight, Jade?' Lenore asked after a minute's awkward silence.

'An outfit for me to wear to the races on Saturday. Whitmore Opals are sponsoring one of the races at Rosehill and it's my job to sash the winning horse. I have to look the part. Kyle says I'm not to embarrass him or the company by wearing something outlandish.'

Jade avoided Lenore's penetrating look, turning her head to window shop. 'This boutique has some nice things in it,' she said, stopping. 'What do you think, Lenore? Do you think that blue dress would suit me?'

'Not if you're dressing for a man.'

'I'm not,' Jade snapped.

'So what happened between you and the marketing manager? Or aren't you ever going to tell me?'

Jade shrugged, her heart sinking as it did whenever she thought of Kyle these days. If only he'd been nasty to her these past few weeks. But no, he'd been exceptionally decent and polite. Remote, though. And strictly business. Her one attempt really to talk to him had been given short shrift, and she hadn't tried again.

'Didn't he fancy you?' Lenore asked gently.

Jade laughed. 'Oh, he fancied me all right, but I was my usual stupid self and gave him the impression that I only wanted him for sex ... which perhaps I did at first. I can see now that his male pride had trouble with that,' she went on shakily. 'Looking back, I think he also became worried that his career at Whitmore's might be jeopardised by sleeping with me. So he cut dead our affair before it had hardly begun.'

Jade had to stop for a second, an enormous lump filling her throat. 'I only realised afterwards,' she choked out, 'how much I ... really loved him, and *needed* him, and ... and ... oh, God, I'm so miserable.'

Jade dissolved into tears right then and there, her shoulders shaking uncontrollably as her head dropped into her hands.

'Oh, you poor love,' Lenore sympathised, putting her arms around her and leading her away to a quiet corner till she could compose herself. Which she eventually did.

'Would you like to marry this man, Jade?' Lenore asked carefully.

Jade nodded.

'Goodness, then you do love him, don't you? You always said marriage was for the birds. And babies? Have you changed your mind about that as well?'

Jade's thinking hadn't carried her that far as yet. She'd always feared she'd make a terrible mother. Now, her mind and heart filled with the images of having Kyle's baby, of holding it in her arms, caring for it, loving it. Something moved deep within her, something warm and strong and elemental.

Oh, what a fool she'd been to think she would not make a good mother. She'd make a *great* mother, because she knew exactly what a child needed most of all. Love.

Her eyes glistened with new tears. 'I'd love to have Kyle's babies. But that's just wishful thinking. He doesn't love me or want to marry me. He never did.'

'You can't be sure of that, Jade. Male pride makes liars out of the best men. Why don't you tell him how you feel and see what happens?'

'Oh, no.' She shook her head vigorously. 'I . . . I couldn't do that.'

'Why not? What have you got to lose?'

'What have I got to lose?' Her smile was infinitely sad. 'His respect. I think, oddly enough, I might have gained some of that in his eyes lately. If I tell him I love him, he'll think I'm trying to blackmail him back into a sexual relationship. I am the boss's daughter, after all. No, Lenore, Kyle's the sort of man who makes his own decisions where women are concerned. If he ever wants me back, he'll let me know.'

'Maybe so,' Lenore returned a little drily. 'But there's no reason why his wanting you back can't be helped along a little, is there?'

'And how can I do that? I have no intention of being obvious, Lenore. *Or* bold. That won't work a second time.'

'My dear, there is no need to be obvious, *or* bold, to be desirable. Come along. We have some shopping to do.'

CHAPTER FOURTEEN

'MY GOD, Jade, what have you done to yourself!' Ava exclaimed. 'I've never seen you look so...so...'

'Exquisite?' Melanie suggested, walking into Ava's studio with the vacuum cleaner in one hand and a duster in the other.

'Yes,' Ava agreed, throwing the housekeeper a ready smile. 'That's the word. Exquisite. And what a sensational figure she has. I'd give my eye-teeth for one half as good.'

Jade was truly taken aback by their compliments. When Lenore had selected an ultra-feminine white lace over organza dress from the racks, her immediate reaction had been negative. Demure clothes didn't suit her, and this dress was demure, with a high neck and long sleeves, not to mention a mid-calf gored skirt.

'You really think it looks all right?' Jade asked, still unsure.

She'd bought the dress on Lenore's say-so, not at all convinced Kyle would like such an old-fashioned looking outfit. Though he had said once he liked her in white. Perhaps it was the white organza picture hat she was uncomfortable with, not to mention the pearl choker and matching earrings. She felt like a member of the royal family going to Ascot, or one of those garden brides at the turn of the century.

'I hope I don't have to walk far,' she muttered. 'These new shoes are going to kill me by the end of the day.'

'They look lovely.'

'They should at the price. In fact, this outfit has set me back a pretty penny, which is ridiculous since I'll never wear it again.'

'You never know,' her aunt soothed. 'Is that a new perfume I can smell?' she asked, coming over to sniff. 'It's very nice.'

Melanie put down the vacuum cleaner to walk over and have a sniff as well.

'Hmm. Very erotic,' was her murmured comment, bringing a sharp look from Jade. The woman had sounded wistful, yet sensual. It wasn't the first time Jade had thought their housekeeper had a strong sexual streak in her.

'What's it called?' Ava asked.

'Desire.'

Melanie lifted her dark eyebrows and turned away to plug in the vacuum cleaner. 'Sorry to put an end to our chat, but I must get on with this. You do look lovely, Jade. I hope your day is a big success.'

'How can it help but be?' Ava said, smiling. 'Jade doesn't have to win the race, only sash the winner and look pretty for the photos. Isn't that right, dear? Now let's go downstairs and show your father how beautiful you look.'

'Do we have to?' Jade groaned.

'You can't,' Melanie said from behind them. 'He's gone out.'

Jade breathed a sigh of relief.

'Darn,' Ava grumbled. 'Where's he gone?'

'To golf.'

'Golf?' He can hardly walk upstairs, let alone around a golf course.'

'He bought one of those driving carts.'

'Truly. Nobody tells me anything around here.'

'He did mention it last night, Auntie,' Jade recalled, 'but you were watching a movie.'

'Oh . . . yes, well, people shouldn't tell me things when I'm watching a movie. You know what I'm like.'

Jade laughed and linked arms with her aunt. 'We certainly do, darls, especially when the movie's a romance.'

'Don't call me that,' the older woman complained. 'I hate it. Frankly, it's high time you stopped using that term altogether. It sounds cheap.'

'Cheap?' Jade was astonished.

'Yes, cheap!'

'Then it won't pass my lips again,' she promised faithfully. 'My days of cheap are over.'

'And about time too!' her aunt announced firmly as they went downstairs.

They were just stepping on to the rug at the bottom of the stairs when the buzzer near the front door announced a visitor wanting entry at the gates. Instant butterflies crowded Jade's stomach as she hurried over to flick the switch on the security intercom.

'Is that you, Kyle?'

'It is.'

'Sorry about the gates. I'll open them for you.'

'Thank you.'

So chillingly polite, she thought, and shivered. Suddenly, the day ahead took on a bleak reality. She should never have listened to Lenore, should never have allowed her hopes to be raised.

Closing her eyes, she just stood there. Her breathing came deep and even as she tried desperately to compose herself, to hide her misery behind a cool calm façade.

'Are you all right, dear?'

Jade swung round, her eyes flying open to see her aunt's concerned face.

'Yes, of course. I was just daydreaming.'

'You like Mr Armstrong, don't you?'

Jade stiffened. 'I admire him. Yes.'

'I see,' the other woman said slowly. 'Well, have a nice time, dear, and we'll see you when we see you.'

The front doorbell rang and Jade went to open the door. Her insides tightened as her eyes swept over the man she loved.

How handsome he looked. That black suit did things for his colouring that no other colour did. And his body did things for the suit in return that not many men's would.

'You're a little early,' she said stiffly.

The corner of his mouth lifted in a small, sardonic smile. 'Maybe I was anxious to see this vision of loveliness.'

Jade froze. Was he mocking her? Or could Lenore have been spot on? 'You...you really like what I'm wearing?'

He seemed surprised by her obvious lack of confidence. 'Don't you?'

'I just didn't think this was me.'

'Well, if it isn't you,' he said drily, 'then, whoever it is, don't bother to change. What you're wearing is perfect.'

Jade could feel the heat gathering in her cheeks. 'I have to get my purse. Do you want to come in?'

'No. I'll wait here.'

Jade hurried upstairs to her room where she snatched up the pearlised clutch purse she'd also bought the other night, then took one last glance in her dressing-table mirror.

'He likes how I look,' she whispered happily. 'He really does.'

Eyes bright with relief and excitement, she came downstairs, trying not to hurry too much. Lenore had insisted she be pleasant, but not too anxious to please. Sweet, but not cloying.

Once on the front patio with the front door closed behind them, Kyle took her elbow and gallantly escorted her down the steps, opening the door for her and seeing her properly seated and belted before striding round to the driver's side. Jade tried hard not to let her gaze follow his every move, but to no avail. She couldn't seem to get enough of him today, even if it was only with her eyes.

'Yes?' he asked after belting himself in and noticing that she was still staring at him.

'Oh... I—er—nothing.' God, but she was hopeless! Lenore would be grimacing, if she could see her now.

Kyle started the car and they were away. Jade focused straight ahead, determined not to move her head an inch his way until they arrived at the racecourse. The silence between them lengthened, the atmosphere becoming terribly tense.

'Jade...' he began at last while they were stopped at a red light.

'Yes?' She kept her eyes on the road ahead.

He sighed irritably. 'This is more damned difficult than I thought it would be.'

'Well, it needn't be,' she suddenly snapped, mortified that she'd started hoping stupid hopes. What a fool she was! 'I realise you're only taking me to the races today because you have to. I'm not under any illusions that this is a date or anything. You told me to get all glammed up so I did. There's no reason for you to feel you have to treat me any differently than you do at the office these days. You've made it perfectly clear you don't want any relationship with me other than a working one, even if I still do, so I...I...'

Jade refused to burst into tears at this juncture but she just couldn't go on. She'd already said far too much. So she simply stopped talking and stared through the passenger window. But it was an unseeing stare. When the car drew to a halt again, she presumed it was because of another red light.

'Jade. Turn round and face me.'

Angry blue eyes whipped round at his demanding tone to find he'd pulled over into a side-street and parked. 'What do you want now?' she snapped again. 'Haven't you done enough yet, Kyle? Must you keep on crucifying me?'

Jade was taken aback by the truly pained look that crossed his face.

'God, is that how bad it's been? I'm truly sorry, my darling. Truly, truly sorry.'

Jade gaped at him. My *darling*? What was going on here? What cruel game was he playing at now?

Suddenly, he unsnapped his seatbelt, leant over and kissed her startled mouth, softly, sweetly. 'I didn't mean to make you suffer,' he murmured, lifting his head, then smiling a faintly sardonic smile. 'Well, I might have... a little... at first. But afterwards, I knew it was the only way I could be sure, the only way I could make you see the truth.'

'What truth?' she asked, utterly confused now.

'That you really loved me. That it wasn't just sex.'

'Of course I really loved you, you stupid man!' she burst forth. 'I knew that! Why didn't you? My God, are you saying you loved me all along? If you are saying that, Kyle Armstrong, then you'd better get out of this car and start running because I...'

He kissed her again, kissed her and told her he loved her over and over till she was crying with joy and relief and so many mixed emotions, not the least of which was total bewilderment.

'I still don't see why you couldn't tell me you loved me before,' she cried.

'The way you told me, perhaps? Think, Jade. What *did* you tell me? That you didn't know what you felt for me except that the sex was great, that you were never going to marry or have children, and that once you learnt my job I was expendable.'

'Oh!' An embarrassed heat crowded her face. 'But I... I didn't realise at that stage how much I loved you!'

'Exactly. You didn't realise because I was confusing you with sex and generally being a precipitate fool. I pulled back, Jade, hoping a break would force you to see the truth. I thought you might be in love with me but I couldn't be sure. I'm sorry if it hurt but I've been hurting too.'

Jade stared at him. 'But I... I might have ended up hating you instead.'

'You didn't, though, did you?' he smiled.

'When... when did you fall in love with me?'

'I think the process began that first night at dinner. Do you remember when I started coughing?'

'Yes... yes, I do.'

'You'd just smiled over at me. Such a sad smile, my darling. It tore at my heart and made me want to take care of you, to comfort you. It came to me then that you were the woman I was going to marry.'

'*Marry*!' she squawked. 'I thought you only lusted after me that first night.'

'That too. I fought both impulses, I can assure you. Told myself that I couldn't possibly bed my boss's outrageous daughter, let alone want to marry her. But my subconscious obviously didn't agree because before I knew it I was contriving to have you work with me, pretending it was for your own good when in fact all I wanted was any excuse to have you around me. God, how I wanted you!'

He laughed softly. 'I did quite well to last till the Friday, don't you think? The straw that broke the camel's back was thinking you might actually go out and go to bed with some other man. I couldn't have that when I knew it was *me* you wanted. I decided then and there to be your next lover, no matter what. But then I found out you were nothing like you pretended to be. Nothing at all! You wcrc swcct and innocent and adorable and I fell for you like a ton of hot bricks.'

'But you very definitely said that night you didn't love me,' Jade recalled, frowning. 'You said you never fell in love.'

'I never have. I've always been a cold, controlled bastard. I've never known love, you see. My parents died when I was just a baby and I was put into a boarding-school when I was a tot. It took a very special person to make me fall in love, Jade, and *still* I didn't recognise the emotion. I knew I liked you and admired you and desired you, but it wasn't till you teased me that day in the office about having no control that I finally saw the truth. You see, I've never not been in control with a woman before.'

Now Jade did frown. 'But why did you back away? I still don't understand...'

'Don't forget what you'd just said to me that day, about never wanting to get married or have children. Not to mention that crack about my being your toy-boy right at the same moment I realised I loved you. You were denying me what I wanted most in the world. *You*, as my wife and the mother of my children. I lashed out in frustration and I'm terribly sorry. I regretted everything immediately I stormed out, but my pride wouldn't let me come back. I was off my head, thinking your only interest in me was carnal.'

'Oh, Kyle...'

'It wasn't till I'd calmed down that I realised you might love me underneath that flighty façade you hide behind, and which I already knew was a lie. I also decided to gamble that your decision about marriage and children was a backlash against your parents' miserable marriage, not to mention your mother's appalling treatment of you. I began to have faith that you really loved me, but I had to convince *you* of that, so I put your love to the test these past few weeks and you came through, darling Jade. *We* came through. We love each other, really love each other. It's not just lust. It's true love. Marry me, darling. Marry me and I'll make you happy, I promise...'

By this time tears were misting Jade's eyes. She reached out and picked up his hands, squeezing them to her heart.

'Oh, yes, Kyle. Yes...'

'And babies?'

'As many as you like.'

The joy on his face moved her so much that more tears followed.

'You don't know how happy you've made me,' he choked out, taking out his pocket handkerchief and wiping her streaming cheeks.

'I've ruined my make-up,' she laughed. 'Do we still have to go to the races?'

'The races! My God, I forgot.' He glanced at his watch. 'We have to go, Jade. I can't let people down like that. Damn, I wanted to... Oh, well, I guess that can wait until tonight...

'I have to confess I'm a little afraid of horses,' Jade nervously told the PR person from the racing authority as the winner of the Whitmore Opal Stakes was brought back to be weighed. Jade eyed the sweating animal with growing temerity as the jockey slid off and they waited round till weight was declared right, after which Kyle made a small speech on behalf of Whitmore Opals and presented the owner with a trophy and an opal ring.

Jade watched, fascinated and admiring, Kyle's absolute composure and confidence. If it had been her up there she would have been umming and aahing everywhere. There again, a man like Kyle only came along once in a million years, she believed. And he was going to be her husband. She sighed with happiness.

'Time to sash the winner now, Miss Whitmore,' the PR man whispered in her ear.

Jade took a deep breath and stepped forward.

'Thank God the poor thing was too tired to do anything but nod,' she said afterwards to Kyle, curling a happy arm through his. 'Can we go home now?'

He smiled down at her. 'My home or yours?'

'Ours.'

'Ours?'

'You did ask me to move in with you, didn't you?' she said. 'How about tonight?'

'I do like the way you make decisions, Ms Whitmore.'

They were just turning away when someone tapped Kyle on the shoulder.

'Kyle? Is that you?'

Both of them whirled round. A striking blonde in bright pink was standing there, giving Kyle a peeved look.

'So it *is* you!' she said, throwing a curious glance Jade's way before returning her gorgeous green eyes to Kyle's stony face. 'Well, what have you got to say for yourself, Mr Gainsford? I've been waiting weeks for you to call as you said you would,' she tripped off, not sounding overly upset. 'Still, I'm not one to hold a grudge. Call me when you get back to Tassie. I'll be waiting. Ta-ta!'

She walked off, waving coyly, the crowd soon swallowing her up.

Jade wished the ground would open and swallow her up as well. She was an intelligent girl and it didn't take long to put two and two together. What a pity four was such a nauseating number. A nauseating, despairing number. With a tormented groan, she lifted distressed eyes to the man standing stiffly beside her.

'Well, Mr Gainsford,' she said shakily, 'or whoever you are—want to tell me what that was all about? Make it good, because there are laws in this state against false representation.'

His expression did not reflect the expression she might have expected on an exposed con-man. He'd become Mr Cool again. Or was it Mr Arrogant?

'For God's sake, Jade,' he ground out. 'You're jumping to all the wrong conclusions. Hell...' His hands raked through his black curls, giving him a less cool image. 'Why did that stupid bitch have to show up today, of all days? And here, of all places!'

'I dare say you slept with her, and conned her too.'

'If anyone was doing the conning on that occasion, it was the lady,' he countered harshly. 'She turned out to be a gold-digger.'

'Well, she struck out with you, didn't she? What happened? Did you use your rich mate's name with her, and she thought it was you with the millions? Yes, of course that's what you did. How silly of me. *You're* the gold-digger this time, though, aren't you? Do tell me, Kyle. Is it me you're after, or the company?'

'Just you.'

She gasped her shock that he could admit such a thing. 'But I'm not that rich!'

'I know that. But *I am*. And my name *is* Gainsford. I'm probably one of the richest men in Australia.'

Jade's head jerked back. '*What*?'

'You don't have to take my word for it. Check me out if you like. But before you put your pretty foot further into your pretty mouth, let me give you the simple facts, the same ones I would have told you before the races, if I'd had time. Hell, I shouldn't have put it off, but I guess I wanted to live the fantasy a little longer.'

Jade blinked, her brain still blank with shock.

Kyle sighed. 'This will probably sound pretty far-fetched but it's the truth. I assumed a false name and false work record to get an ordinary job and live an ordinary life, because I wanted to find a woman who would love me for who I am, not what I owned.'

Jade blinked some more.

'God!' He pulled her to him, his grip unyielding, black eyes blazing with a dark passion. 'Do you hear what I'm saying? I wanted to get married and have a family, and I wanted my wife to really truly love me. Me, the man, not me, Mr Moneybags. Well, I found her. And I love her like mad, and I'm not going to let her go. Not ever. Believe me when I say that, even if you don't believe anything else.'

Jade was still having trouble taking it all in, though there was no doubting Kyle's sincerity. But what an amazing, incredible story! Perhaps she should have been angry with him for such a deception, but instead she was deeply moved. Kyle's upbringing sounded as awful as her own. And just as lacking in love. No wonder they'd been drawn to each other.

'There's no mysterious Mr Gainsford, then?' she asked. 'You're him?'

'I am.'

'Then that night on the houseboat... You were talking about yourself?'

He nodded and she remembered all that he had said about not liking the man he'd been once, but liking him more now.

'Why did you choose Armstrong?' she asked, still a little dazed.

'It's my secretary's surname.'

'Your... your secretary?'

'My secretary's a man, before you jump to any more false conclusions,' he added drily. 'It was he who rang me at the office that day, not a woman.'

'Oh...' She frowned up at him as a thought struck. 'If you're so rich, why doesn't your name ring a bell?'

'My parents were American.'

'I thought you were Tasmanian?'

'I am. When I was born my parents received a kidnap threat which they took seriously. They emigrated to Tasmania, where they bought a secluded country property, thinking they'd be safe. But that was in 1967, the year of Tasmania's worst bushfire. They perished in it, but somehow I survived, heir at six months old to billions of dollars. I grew up being given everything but love, Jade. And over the years, I tried everything but love. Then one day I saw the emptiness of my life and knew what I had to do. I came looking for love. And I found it.'

Jade felt like crying, till she thought of something. 'Does my father know all this?'

'Not a word of it.'

'Goodness. He's going to be furious with you for deceiving him.'

'Let's not tell him just yet. I like working at Whitmore's, Jade. I'd like to see if together we can really rescue the place and make it a success.'

'Oh, yes, I'd like that. But he's still going to be furious when we eventually tell him.'

'Not if you present him with a son-in-law and a grandchild.'

'A grandchild?'

'I want a family, Jade, and I want it soon.'

'I... I still want a career at Whitmore's, Kyle.'

'Of course you do. Of course! I would never ask you to give up your life's dream. I'll help all I can. And I think I can afford a nanny or two, don't you?' he added, smiling.

Jade thought of the pills she'd thrown away after that awful incident at the office and her heart squeezed tight. 'We could start trying tonight, if you like.'

He seemed startled. 'You mean that, Jade? You've still got this year to go at uni.'

'True... Well, perhaps we should only practise for a month or two, before we try to hit a home run.'

Kyle laughed and hugged her. 'I do so love you.'

'You'd better,' she warned. 'And soon. I've been going mad, missing you.'

'*You've* been going mad! Tell you what, I'll race you to the car.'

'Don't be ridiculous, Kyle,' she reproached. 'Have some decorum.'

While he was looking suitably chastened, she slipped off her shoes and made a dash for it, whooping as she went.

Kyle swore and took off after her. He should have known white lace hadn't made her into a lady. But then, he didn't want a lady, did he? He wanted his Jade.

He began to run faster.

CHAPTER FIFTEEN

AVOCA beach was fairly deserted, partly because it was Monday, but mostly because the weather had turned nasty overnight. A southerly change had blown in a couple of minutes after midnight, bringing with it freezing winds from the Antarctic. Gemma knew the exact moment the change had struck, because she'd been wide awake in her bed. Wide awake and alone. Again.

Tucking her hands under her arms, she put her head down and kept walking along the sand, hoping the sharp breeze would brush away the cobwebs from her mind so that it could focus on reality rather than romantic fantasy. Had she expected too much from her marriage? Had she painted Nathan in her mind as some sort of god, and not a human being with human failings?

She stopped, and stared out to sea, her hair whipping across her face, salt-spray stinging her eyes. The water was very choppy, the waves building as the tide came in. A walk around the rocks was out of the question. Only a madman would do that. Or a potential suicide.

Gemma shuddered, then frowned. Fancy thinking such a thing! Things weren't as bad as that! Every newly married couple had adjustments to make, especially once the honeymoon was over.

But the honeymoon *shouldn't* be over yet, an inner voice niggled. You've only been married two and half weeks. Just because Nathan's doing a little writing...

A *little*? that insidious voice scorned. That was the understatement of the year!

She'd woken in the early hours of yesterday morning feeling cold, only to find Nathan's side of the bed empty. Slipping a robe over her naked body, she'd gone in search of her husband, trying the kitchen first. But it too was empty. Maybe he was in the bathroom. She was walking back to the bedroom when she'd noticed the light under the den door at the end of the hallway.

Relieved, she'd hurried down and gone in, startled to find a fully dressed Nathan sitting at his computer, tapping away like a man possessed. Despite her abrupt entry, he'd kept typing away for at least a minute before looking up and snapping, 'What?'

'I . . . I was wondering where you were?'

'Well, now you know. I'm in here and, as you can see, I'm working.'

Gemma was so stunned by his brusque manner that she just stood there, speechless.

'Go back to bed,' he ordered, his eyes already back on the screen, his fingers flying over the keys. 'And close the door on your way out.'

She'd retreated, telling herself over and over that it was absurd to feel so hurt. He hadn't meant anything personally. He'd been preoccupied, that was all. She'd known he was a writer when she married him. Kirsty had often spoken of his obsessiveness when creating, so she'd even been warned about it.

Determined not to let things flare out of all proportion, she'd made herself a hot drink and gone back to bed, feeling confident that Nathan would join her later. Now they were married, he didn't seem able to stay away from her for long, wanting to make love morning, noon and night. Yes, no doubt he'd join her long before breakfast.

But he hadn't joined her. Gemma had woken shortly before nine, still alone. And worse was yet to come. Nathan had stayed in that damned room all Sunday, scowling at her the one time she'd dared enter to bring him a tray of food.

'I can't stop to eat now,' she'd been told, his tone irritable and exasperated. 'Oh, just leave it. I'll have something shortly. Why don't you go for a walk? Or a swim? I *have* to finish this scene, Gemma. I shouldn't be much longer.'

By Sunday evening, Gemma's mood had swung from distress to depression. Was this what marriage to Nathan was going to be like from now on, long lonely hours stretching into even longer lonelier days and nights? How would she fill her time? Nathan didn't want her to work or have children for a couple of years, saying a couple had to get to know each other before they introduced a baby into their lives.

Getting to know each other...

Gemma had mulled over that thought all Sunday evening. She didn't really know Nathan any better today than she had on their wedding-day. How could that be when they'd spent every minute of every day together up till now?

The truth was they'd done little else except eat, sleep and make love. Physically, they'd become attuned as Nathan had said they would, and yes, he only had to look at her a certain way to spark her own increasingly demanding desires. But was such sexual intimacy *real* intimacy? She wanted to know Nathan's mind, as well as his body, and vice versa.

Gemma had finally fallen asleep on the Sunday night, feeling unhappy and disturbed. When she'd woken the following morning, still alone, a surge of anger had seized her and before she could think better of it she'd flounced down to that infernal room and walked right in.

Nathan had been sprawled on the sofa, sound asleep.

Her anger evaporating, she had sighed and shaken her head, for he looked rather sweet and vulnerable, lying there like that, his hair dishevelled and a five o'clock shadow on his chin. He'd also looked cold, his knees drawn up in a foetal position, his arms wrapped around himself. Smiling softly, she had collected a blanket from the spare bedroom and spread it over him, bending to smooth that wayward lock of hair from his forehead. He'd moaned softly and turned over. So had her heart. Dear lord, but she loved him so much. What a fool she was to get herself all worked up over his writing for a day or two! As for their getting to know one another... They had their whole lives to do that.

She had been tiptoeing out when she spied the messy printer read-out all over on the floor. Now wasn't that just like a man? Shaking her head, she'd gone over and tidied up the pages, and had been about to put them on the corner of the desk next to the computer when the title of the play jumped out at her.

In Darkness He Stirs.

Intrigued, she had been about to start reading further when the pages were snatched out of her hands and thrown into a nearby chair. 'Nobody reads what I write unless I ask them to,' Nathan snarled, glaring at her with cold fury.

She simply stared up at him, eyes wide, a trembling deep inside. Her father had looked at her like that. Often.

Suddenly, Nathan groaned, and grabbed her to him, embracing her fiercely. 'Don't look at me like that,' he said huskily. 'God, I'm sorry. I didn't mean it. Always remember that, Gemma. When I'm writing, I'm not myself.'

He held her away from him then, his eyes dark and haunted. 'Tell me you understand, Gemma. Tell me you don't mind. It would kill me if you minded, because I *have* to write. I simply have to.'

'It's all right, Nathan,' she lied. 'I...I don't mind.'

'I've been neglecting you, I know,' he growled, cupping her chin with a less than tender hand. 'I don't mean to. I'll make it up to you. I won't be much longer, darling. After I've finished this next act we'll be together again.' He kissed her, quite passionately, then sent her away, unfulfilled and aching for him.

That had been six hours ago. In the end, unable to stand the house any longer, Gemma had walked down to the shops and bought herself an ice-cream, then gone down to the beach, hoping to make some sense of the storm gathering inside her.

A gust of wind hit and she shivered. I'll have to go back, she thought wretchedly. Back to that horrible house.

Gemma didn't go back straight away, however. As she passed the old picture theatre, she noticed a session was about to start so she went in. At the back of her mind she knew she was only delaying a possible confrontation between herself and Nathan, plus their first marital argument. But she was only human, and the thought of conflict upset her.

So she sat for the next couple of hours and watched one of those mindlessly violent action movies where the hero looked like an overmuscled freak and couldn't act to save himself. She counted forty-four corpses and left the theatre, feeling like one herself.

Taking a deep breath, she set off up the hill and was labouring up their steep driveway when Nathan burst out on to the front veranda, looking like the hounds of hell were after him. 'Gemma! Where on earth have you been? I've been looking everywhere for you!' He came racing down the steps, grabbing her shoulders and looking her over as though expecting to find bullet holes in her. 'I've been worried sick. I searched everywhere and couldn't find you. I was just about to call the police.'

Oddly enough, his frantic concern irritated her. 'Really?' She pushed past him and marched up the steps and into the front living-room. 'I was at a movie, if you must know,' she threw back over her shoulder, sensing him behind her.

When he grabbed her and spun her round she was about to lash out some more when he yanked her hard against him, holding her head against his loudly thudding heart. 'You don't understand. I thought you might have gone round the rocks. I thought... hell, I thought so many things. If anything ever happened to you, I'd die, Gemma.'

'You weren't too worried about me while you were writing,' Gemma said in a voice she could hardly believe had come from her. It sounded cynical and bitter. But, having started, she didn't seem able to stop. 'You might as well know right from the start, Nathan. I have no intention of living the rest of my life like this.'

Nathan released her abruptly, and stepped back, staring down at her. 'You're leaving me,' he stated, looking appalled, yet sounding oddly resigned.

His face and words stunned her. Yet, in a weird way, they totally defused her anger. Was this what happened to a person after they'd gone through a divorce? Gemma shook her head in disbelief that he would even *think* such a thing.

'Of *course* I'm not leaving you! I was talking about my going to work, Nathan. You might not realise this but I was very disappointed about that, especially after mastering my basic Japanese. I might not be a genius but I do have a mind and I do get bored, especially when you leave me alone as long as you have these past two days. I understand you need to write. It's part of who you are. But I can't just sit around all day doing nothing.'

Nathan's smile was a mixture of relief and joy as he swept her back into his arms. 'Of course you can't, darling. Of course. I've been very selfish. It's only logical that you'd want to work, a smart girl like you. Look, I'll buy us a unit near town. We'll live down there during the week and up here at the weekends.'

'That sounds wonderful,' Gemma murmured, a little dazed at how quickly Nathan had resolved what could have become a big problem between them.

'It *will* be wonderful,' he reassured, 'because I have a wonderful wife and if I ever forget that again I hope she'll keep reminding me.'

Gemma smiled softly and reached up to rub Nathan's bristly chin. 'You need a shave.'

'And a bath. Care to join me?'

Her eyes rounded, yet she shouldn't have been surprised. Already Nathan had brought her round to a lot of activities she might once have found shocking. 'You're a wicked man,' she teased, though a little breathlessly.

His eyes narrowed on to her mouth. 'You could be right,' he muttered, and bent to kiss her. 'Did you miss me?' he rasped against her lips.

'Yes.'

'Do you want me?'

'Yes.'

'Tell me you love me?'

'I love you.'

He groaned, and, sweeping her up into his arms, carried her down towards the bathroom.

HARLEQUIN ◆ PRESENTS®

Dark secrets...
forbidden desires...
scandalous discoveries...
an enthralling six-part saga from a bright new talent!

HEARTS OF FIRE
by Miranda Lee

This exciting new family saga is set in the glamorous world of opal dealing in Australia. *HEARTS OF FIRE* unfolds over six books, revealing the passion, scandal, sin and hope that exist between two fabulously rich families. Each novel features its own gripping romance—and you'll also be hooked by the continuing story of Gemma Smith's search for the truth about her real mother, and the priceless Black Opal....

Coming next month
BOOK 3: *Passion & the Past*

After the tragic end to her marriage, Melanie was sure she could never feel for any man again—until Royce Grantham set his blue eyes on her! Melanie was determined not to repeat past mistakes...but Royce made her feel overwhelmed by desire. Meanwhile, Nathan's trusting young bride, Gemma, had already been seduced by passion—and was discovering the difference between lust and love....

Harlequin Presents: you'll want to know what happens next!

Available in September wherever Harlequin books are sold.

FIRE3

MILLION DOLLAR SWEEPSTAKES (III)

HARLEQUIN PRESENTS®

Ever felt the excitement of a dangerous desire...?

The thrill of a feverish flirtation...?

Passion is guaranteed with the third in our new selection of
sensual stories.

Indulge in...

Dangerous Liaisons

Falling in love is a risky affair!

Look out next month for:

Shades of Sin

by SARA WOOD

Harlequin Presents #1765

The rebel is back! Four years ago, Natasha had fallen
for the local "bad boy," Ruan Gardini. He'd made Natasha
come alive for the first time...but it was a turbulent
relationship and they'd parted bitter enemies. Now Ruan
was back to claim his revenge for the sins of the past, and
he was every bit as daring, sexy and irresistible as
Natasha remembered!

Available in September wherever Harlequin books are sold.

As a *Privileged Woman,*
you'll be entitled to all
these *Free Benefits.*
And *Free Gifts,* too.

To thank you for buying our books, we've designed an exclusive FREE program called *PAGES & PRIVILEGES™*. You can enroll with just one Proof of Purchase, and get the kind of luxuries that, until now, you could only read about.

*B*IG HOTEL DISCOUNTS

A privileged woman stays in the finest hotels. And so can you—at up to 60% off! Imagine standing in a hotel check-in line and watching as the guest in front of you pays $150 for the same room that's only costing you $60. Your *Pages & Privileges* discounts are good at Sheraton, Marriott, Best Western, Hyatt and thousands of other fine hotels all over the U.S., Canada and Europe.

*F*REE DISCOUNT TRAVEL SERVICE

A privileged woman is always jetting to romantic places. When *you* fly, just make one phone call for the lowest published airfare at time of booking—<u>or double the difference back!</u> PLUS— you'll get a $25 voucher to use the first time you book a flight AND <u>5% cash back on every ticket you buy thereafter through the travel service!</u>

HP-PP4A

𝓕REE GIFTS!

A privileged woman is always getting wonderful gifts.
Luxuriate in rich fragrances that will stir your senses (and his). This gift-boxed assortment of fine perfumes includes three popular scents, each in a beautiful designer bottle.   Truly Lace...This luxurious fragrance unveils your sensuous side. L'Effleur...discover the romance of the Victorian era with this soft floral. Muguet des bois...a single note floral of singular beauty.

YOURS FREE!

$50 VALUE

𝓕REE INSIDER TIPS LETTER

A privileged woman is always informed. And you'll be, too, with our free letter full of fascinating information and sneak previews of upcoming books.

𝓜ORE GREAT GIFTS & BENEFITS TO COME

A privileged woman always has a lot to look forward to. And so will you. You get all these wonderful FREE gifts and benefits now with only one purchase...and there are no additional purchases required. However, each additional retail purchase of Harlequin and Silhouette books brings you a step closer to even more great FREE benefits like half-price movie tickets... and even more FREE gifts.

*L'Effleur...*This basketful of romance lets you discover L'Effleur from head to toe, heart to home.

Truly Lace...
A basket spun with the sensuous luxuries of Truly Lace, including Dusting Powder in a reusable satin and lace covered box.

Complete the Enrollment Form in the front of this book and mail it with this Proof of Purchase.

PROOF OF PURCHASE
Offer expires October 31, 1996

HP-PP4